Also by Joseph Scapellato

Big Lonesome

THE MADE-UP MAN

THE MADE-UP MAN

Joseph Scapellato

WITHDRAWN

Farrar, Straus and Giroux   New York

Farrar, Straus and Giroux
175 Varick Street, New York 10014

Printed in the United States of America
First edition, 2019

Library of Congress Cataloging-in-Publication Data
Names: Scapellato, Joseph, 1982– author.
Title: The made-up man / Joseph Scapellato.
Description: First edition. | New York : Farrar, Straus and Giroux, [2019]
Identifiers: LCCN 2018033299 | ISBN 9780374200077 (hardcover)
Subjects: LCSH: Psychological fiction.
Classification: LCC PS3619.C2666 M33 2019 | DDC 813/.6—dc23
LC record available at https://lccn.loc.gov/2018033299

Designed by Jonathan D. Lippincott

Our books may be purchased in bulk for promotional, educational, or
business use. Please contact your local bookseller or the Macmillan Corporate
and Premium Sales Department at 1-800-221-7945, extension 5442, or by
e-mail at MacmillanSpecialMarkets@macmillan.com.

www.fsgbooks.com
www.twitter.com/fsgbooks • www.facebook.com/fsgbooks

10 9 8 7 6 5 4 3 2 1

for made-up men and women

Archaeology is destruction.
—archaeologists

PART I

ONLY THE STUPID
CAN BE HAPPY

1

Stanley Arrives in Prague

The man who met me at the airport was made up. He wore concealer and low-key lipstick. On both hands, his fingernails had been lacquered in clear polish. I was meant to notice these unsubtle subtleties, which I did, and I was meant to feel dropped at the front door to a dark, deviant, and complicated mystery, which I didn't.

"I am representative of your uncle," he said, presenting me the key to the apartment.

He was stooped and saggy-faced, a man dragged all the way to the end of middle age. English sounded hairy in his mouth. He wore a black suit, shirt, and tie, but his sleeve cuffs were streaked with white chalk. The chalk, still powdery, poofed when he moved.

He held a poster-board sign that read:

STANLEY?

and included an impressionistic charcoal portrait of a figure that was meant to be me. No white chalk was in it. The way the face was arranged, it looked about to eat itself.

On the intercom a woman spoke in sternly bored Czech. We were standing near the exit, under the airport's huge hangar-like ceiling. I felt sore and foul from the long flight.

Around us, backpackers, traveling retirees, and businesspeople tapped out cigarettes on their way to the street, where they stopped to smoke, the gathered cloud looming up above them like a ledge full of gargoyles.

"We are thanking you," said the man.

I took the key from his palm. He stared at me with an exaggerated indifference, as if he wanted me to suspect that he was masking spite, as if his goal, outside of key-delivery, was to make me think myself observant. There was a chance I'd seen him in Chicago sometime, slinking out of my uncle's garage with the other artists. To tell them apart was tricky: their work was to change who they were.

He said, "Are you having question?"

My eyes adjusted to his face: its texture shifted, seeming caked and rubbery. He was maybe more made up than I'd thought. I imagined what it would be like to be him—a willing "representative of" my uncle, an adult who'd agreed to participate in another adult's game of pretend—and what I found myself feeling, instead of pity, was disgust. There were many hateful things I could've said to this man. But if I said them, I might shout them, and if I shouted them, I might shove him. It would be the mess my uncle wanted. I put the key in my pocket.

"I won't have questions," I said.

He lowered the sign. His face jerked. "You will find yourself around?"

I left—I crossed the lobby, I went through the doors. Outside I paused in the smoker's cloud to study my map. The urge to smoke was a stake in my chest. I breathed indulgently.

The made-up man watched me from inside the airport, acting like I couldn't see him. He had put a hand to the glass. He was crying.

A bus took me to a tram that took me to the city center. It worked the way the guidebook said it would. From there I walked, and the closer I came to Old Town Square, the more the tourists, travelers, and citizens clotted up the cobblestoned streets and corners, stuck together with their separate languages. Buildings stacked on the centuries, each one older than the last. The streets narrowed and twisted. Through intersections I caught glimpses of the Square, its broad spaces, its mob, its murmur.

The alley that led to where my uncle had said the main door to the apartment was, though, I couldn't find—I went up and down the same set of streets; I squeezed past the same sidewalk cafés and tour guide stands. The alley wasn't where it should have been.

I widened my search, walking bigger boxes-within-boxes.

The streets re-straightened. Tourist spillage shrank. Locals strode into grocery stores and pharmacies, out of banks and boutiques. They plodded up to their apartments above storefronts. I paused at the open door to a butcher shop, where men and women waited in ordinary boredom. An old man paid for a package of hog guts, and a young woman motioned for a bigger hunk of pork, and a little boy kicked another little boy in the butt.

I didn't want to, but I started to double back to the Square. At a corner that I thought I'd recognize, but didn't, I stopped. I stood through several cycles of traffic lights. Citizens coursed by on foot, not speaking, and in cars and on scooters, not honking. I shifted my bag to my other shoulder.

More people passed, their faces firm.

I didn't know what to say to myself: I was afraid.

A fashionable old woman came to a stop in front of me. She glared. I glared back. She looked like the sort of old woman who completed every task on her own, who maintained her solidity through an unreflective commitment to routine. My being there had bent that routine.

She spoke Czech. Her voice was loud and wet.

I told her, in Czech, that I didn't speak Czech, did she speak English?

The light changed again. She snatched my arm and made me help her cross the street, scolding me, shaming me, and at the opposite corner she tried to tug me off-course, her way. I blushed. When I wriggled my arm free, she raised her voice.

People slowed to watch.

She poked me in the chest, yelling now. Her hands had a pickled stink.

A young mother carrying a kid in a body-sling intervened.

The two spoke. The kid squirmed to get a look at my face. He was mustached in snot.

The young mother squinted at me and said something.

I asked her if she spoke English.

"She is saying you are a relative," she said.

"I'm not."

"You look as if you are from here."

"I'm not."

"I am seeing that."

They turned their backs on me together.

For a moment, I didn't move or speak. I couldn't. My fear had peeled away to panic. All of my reasons for being in Prague went bad at once. This was a separate country, a separate people. These were Czechs building Czech lives in a Czech city, thinking and feeling Czech. They themselves were their own reasons for where they were.

A man slammed my bag as he walked by.

The panic crumbled. My mouth was dry, my face was sweaty.

I wandered back the way I'd come.

Near the Square I found the alley I'd been looking for, the entrance shadowed by a busted archway. It could've been a path to a private courtyard. I'd passed it I didn't know how many times. The alley ran straight to my uncle's three-story apartment building, which stood with a sullen pride, shoulder-to-shoulder with its more dignified neighbors. It was wall-like. No first-floor windows, a door that looked like it'd been installed that day. I double-checked the address. The key fit the lock when I jammed and wrenched it. I walked through the lobby and took noisy stairs to the third floor, every step a wincing creak.

The apartment stank a little, a kind of pesticidal sweat worked into the living room, the kitchen, the bedroom. The bed was a full, its sheets coarse to the touch. When I sat on the living room couch the cushions gave out a muffled toot. I slumped. My body deadened, going heavy, and at the same time, my head loosened, going light. It wasn't even noon. I stood up, just to stand up.

That was when a window in me broke.

What broke it came through it: a very bad feeling.

I sat down. The very bad feeling sat down too.

I decided not to think about it.

Stanley Thinks About It

The very bad feeling hadn't been hurled through the window in me by the made-up man or the fashionable old woman. It wasn't the work of panic. It had no connection to jet lag or culture shock, or to recent sleeplessness, or to an old grade of anger that was being hammered into guilt and buffed into dread. It didn't originate in any of the members of my family. It wasn't T—it wasn't anything I hadn't already thought about T, felt about T, and done or not done to T. I put my hands on top of my head. I didn't know what it was.

3

Stanley Knows What It Was

It was a space at the center of myself that wasn't me.

Stanley Tries to Feel the Space at the Center of Himself That Isn't Him

The space at the center of myself that wasn't me had shoved whatever it was that should have been there—my actual center, a central me—flat up against the outlines of myself. I could smell my own stupid breath. The space took up space it had no claim to. It was impenetrable. I couldn't understand it: it was in me, but not me.

I lay on the couch, dizzied. My borders began to warp.

Memories of awful things I'd felt as a kid came crowding back:

Me stomping barefoot on a dead baby bird on accident.

Me slugging a best friend in the face on purpose.

Me hearing my dad trip down the basement stairs, thumping and slapping and shouting hate.

Me seeing my mom raise the chair she'd been sitting on as if to smash it, only to lower it, sit again, and smile.

Me helping Busia from the living room couch to her walker so incorrectly that she slapped me in the throat.

Me and my brother hiding in the bathroom while my brother explained with a calm that I despised how our parents weren't divorcing but weren't planning on spending time together anymore, and although they'd say separately that it wasn't our fault, he knew, for reasons he'd made a list of, that we were to blame.

"Look," he'd said, pressing the list into my hand.

Downstairs our dad yelled, sounding armed, and our mom laughed, sounding armored. They took their act from the kitchen to the living room, from the living room to the dining room, from the dining room to the kitchen. Whoever veered out of character first, lost.

Our dad kicked the stove and hollered.

Our mom clapped out ovations.

My brother said, "Read the list!"

He was at the end of junior high and I was at the end of elementary school. He didn't hide his crying, or couldn't.

I took the matches off the toilet tank and I burned the list in the sink.

My brother didn't smack me—I didn't know it at the time, but he never would again. He put his hand on my shoulder like we were in a movie and we'd made it to the end. He felt better, I saw, and from behind that feeling, he couldn't see that I felt worse. The paper flared and crumpled, smoking. We watched it go out on its own.

Stanley Hears Footsteps, Which, for Reasons That Aren't Clear to Him, Remind Him of His Father

Someone was tromping up the apartment building staircase.

I hadn't left the couch—I felt shaky.

The footsteps were tired and loud. They seemed to say: Get it over with, already. Every major structural component of the staircase—the stringers, the risers, the treads—contracted with rickety squeals, as if the thing had been built to be installed in a haunted house.

I rolled over onto my side, to turn my back to the door.

The footsteps pounded on.

Stanley Reflects on His Decision to Accept His Uncle Lech's Proposal to "Apartment-Sit" for Three Days in Prague

It would be a mistake. I would make it. I would follow through on it.

There would be no mystery in the "mystery" manufactured by my uncle's art project.

There would be nothing I didn't "realize until it was too late."

There would be nothing I didn't "realize until it was too late" with T.

What there would be, instead, was refusal—the refusal to recognize the extent to which I'd lied to myself about the sort of man I wasn't.

Stanley Reflects on the Sort of Man He Was

Before I dated T, I dated Bernadette. We met a month after Ro and I broke up, in early August. That summer I'd been part-timing for my dad's residential remodeling crews, reverse-commuting to south Chicagoland sites where I gophered for subcontractors, fetching tools from trucks and taking lunch orders. It was the job I'd had in high school. On the days I didn't work, I stayed in: I reread old anthropology textbooks, or grunted through a sequence of sit-ups and push-ups and pull-ups, or smoked cigarettes on the stoop, or sat with a six-pack of tallboys in front of the History Channel, which I punched on when I lurched out of bed, dazed, and off when I lurched back, blunted. I kept my apartment tidy, wiping the counters and changing the sheets, but despite my scrubbing and wash-ing and spraying, every room in the place smelled stale. It was like I lived with a roommate I never saw. The only decorations were on the fridge: although it'd been a month since I'd talked to Ro, I hadn't removed the strip of photo booth pictures, the four-shot sequence from her little brother's wedding back in April—Ro in a feather boa and me in a fedora, a couple of crazy poses, a happy cockeyed kiss. I decided that when I could go a day and a night without looking at those pictures, I was over it.

One afternoon, Torrentelli and Barton buzzed up. They'd

bought tickets to the Sox game. "If you don't say yes," said Torrentelli through the intercom, "we'll keep asking until you do." "I have a taser," said Barton. I put on a shirt. We took the Red Line, hanging from hand straps, sharing shitty whiskey from a flask. Residential and industrial cityscapes slashed by. A few stops from Sox Park, a hip kid jumped up on a seat, introduced himself to the car as Criminal A, and broke out into an original rap. Two teenage girls put money in his hat. At the ballpark we hiked to our seats in the empty middle of an upper section. It was late summer, the air exhausted, heavy with humidity. A chemical glow hazed up from the field. In it, the players seemed small, but their actions were big, fast, decisive. I was envious. We burped through beers and a box of nachos. Torrentelli patted my arm and said, "She'll regret it." I didn't even shake my head. Barton gestured at our DH: he struck out swinging, stranding two base runners. "Stop feeling sorry for yourself, and start feeling sorry for your team," he said. We smashed four home runs, all solo shots, but by the seventh-inning stretch we were losing, and in the end we lost by five. We shuffled out of the stadium with the rest of the fans, every one of us having agreed to act like there'd never been a moment when we thought we'd win. A face-painted superfan in a wheelchair chanted, "We won't be good until I'm dead, we won't be good until I'm dead!" The L shot us back to the North Side. We settled on a neighborhoody bar we'd never been to and couldn't find the name of, where we split pitchers and played shuffleboard, misremembering the dangerous things we'd done together growing up and debating the course of the city's future and avoiding the subject of romantic relationships. At last call we shot good whiskey. On the street we decided we weren't done, so we went around the corner to the new 4 a.m. bar, McGrabbits. Until the week before it'd been an unhappy pool hall. The only change was that the tables had been hauled away. The main room was wide and deep and dim, slopped with wasted men and women. The DJ at the back banged from

'90s hip-hop to EDM to remixed classic rock. I was no longer drinking: I was dumping beers into the drain that was my body. Everybody leaned on everybody else, having lost the power to look, move, or act like who they were, and I shouted, "Ro and me are on my fridge!" and Torrentelli shouted, "You don't want to get over her!" and Barton shouted, "You're an asshole, an asshole can get over anybody, anytime, except himself!" and we did a shot of Malört, which even at that hour tasted like licking wood glue off a carpet. Torrentelli left with a bow-tie-wearing hipster prince. Barton shook two cigarettes at me. I promised to close my tab and be right out—I staggered through the stacks of people, clipping shoulders and hips. You're not looking for a fight, I said to myself. You're looking for somebody who's looking for a fight. At the bar I leaned, wallet out. A blue-haired bartender paused in front of me to pour four shots of pink booze. She was as angry as she was bored. I couldn't believe it—her crooked scowl, together with her dye job, made her look like Cassie, my first high school girlfriend, the only woman to ever hit me in the face. Cassie had tic-tac-toed her arms in cuts and polka-dotted her thighs in burns. Anytime she smiled, she made it seem on accident. Our breakup had been a roll across a barbed-wire fence. The bartender slammed the bottle back into a bin. I stared, wanting her to see me, wanting her to mistake me for someone I wasn't, a someone she'd once been sure she'd loved. I waved. I waved at her with both hands. Behind me, a woman said, "You're *aggressive!*" I turned—the woman was short, so short I almost missed her, and dressed for a much fancier event, a corporate benefit or an awards ceremony. Her smile was sincerely drunk. "Get me a drink," she said. I asked her what she wanted. "No," she said, "say, 'What the *fuck* do you want.'" I shifted back to the bar, but she snatched my wrist—her hands were strong. "Are you actually aggressive?" she said. She swung my arm from side to side, the beginning of a kid's game. "I don't know," I said.

I kissed her.

At noon the next day we woke in my bed, pantsless but not shirtless.

"Bernadette," she said.

I brewed coffee. She drank two cups, fast, while I scrambled eggs and Krakus ham.

"Ouch," she kept saying.

I offered her aspirin. She chewed two nonchewable capsules.

"I know what I'm doing," she said. "I'm going to be a doctor-nurse."

She explained that she was about to begin her final year of a PhD in nursing. When she first went into nursing, she said, she wanted to help patients, but before long, she realized that who she really wanted to help were her fellow nurses. We ate standing in the kitchen. While she spoke, she seemed under twenty-one; while she listened, over thirty-five. She was just as short as she'd been the night before.

"With that hat, you look like a private eye," she said, tapping at the photos of me and Ro. "A real 'dick.'"

I set the dishes in the sink.

"Do you have a career?" she said.

I said I'd be starting grad school next week—anthropology, a concentration in archaeology.

She'd been bored until right then.

"You want to be an archaeologist!" she said, impressed. "Tell me why."

"I've wanted to be one since I was a kid."

"Yes. But why?"

I said I didn't know.

She laughed. "That's your motto, 'I don't know, I don't know.'"

"I know I have a reason. It's there—I feel it. I just don't know what it is yet."

"I don't believe you," she said. "You either know the

reason or you don't have one. That's the type of guy you are, I can tell."

I told her that it'd taken me three colleges and six and a half years to twist through to the other side of undergrad. I'd emptied plenty of time into thinking that I knew what my reasons were for transferring to this or that school, for trusting this or that professor's guidance, for declaring this or that major, for pursuing or maintaining or ending this or that romantic relationship. But the truth was that I hadn't known my reasons. What I'd done was mislabel them, consistently. I'd needed to believe that pretending to know what I was doing was the first step to knowing what I was doing.

"I want to be more careful," I said. "I want to know what I'm saying."

Bernadette wrapped herself up in my arm in such a way that I had to put down my coffee.

"We could get to know each other," she said.

Stanley Hears More Footsteps, Then Doors

Whoever had been plodding up the staircase turned off on my floor.

I was still flopped out on the couch.

This person walked the hallway, the footsteps big, angry, booming. He or she stopped at what sounded like the door across from mine. A bag thumped down.

The door unlocked. It juddered open.

The bag was picked back up and the unit was entered.

As soon as the door closed, though, a door farther down the hallway opened with a slow croak.

Then shut with a whoosh and a clap.

When it shut, another door from another part of the hallway whinnied open.

It closed—another opened.

This went on, doors opening and closing, one at a time, as if they were all connected to a single system of interlinked hinges, their swinging and moaning and scraping and banging a demonstration of that system's power, until it seemed that every door to every unit had had its turn except for mine.

Without meaning to, I'd sat up on the couch. I watched the door.

A decisive silence.

I lay down again, this time on my face.

Stanley Continues to Reflect on the Sort of Man He Was

Bernadette and I did dinners and movies and study dates. She spent a Saturday at Taste of Polonia with me and my brother, even though she didn't like ethnically themed festivals, and I spent a weekend with her and her work friends at a fancy lakehouse in Michigan, even though I didn't like fancy lakehouses or her work friends. Once or twice we went to dinner at each other's families' houses. If she was upset and venting, I learned, she expected me to pretend she wasn't, which I found frustrating, and if I was upset but silent, she learned, I expected her to ask me what was up, which she found ridiculous. Mostly we watched true-crime TV.

Later that fall, Bernadette submitted her dissertation to her committee. Because she worked full-time at a hospital, she'd pulled a month's worth of off-day all-nighters to finish it. Excited, she planned a big party at Moody's Pub, setting it on the date of her dissertation defense. She was sure she'd pass.

When the day came, she didn't.

I went straight to her apartment, where she paced, trying to stomp down her resentment. She kicked a hard copy of the dissertation across the floor. Her advisor, a man she'd trusted, had called her work "intentionally incomplete." I sat on a fluffy rug between her two pillow-shaped dogs, Mango and Coconut. She opened a dresser drawer, shoved her face into her folded underwear, and screamed. Her dogs scuttled out of the room, spooked. My sympathy rerouted to revulsion.

"Don't," she said, meaning: Don't think that you can comfort me.

She didn't want her family to know she'd failed her defense, so we trudged to Moody's. The front room filled up with aunts and uncles and cousins from the old country, who brought gifts and cards, and with work friends from across the city, who brought cheers and shouts and party drugs. Bernadette performed Successful Bernadette. I stood by the cake, under the WHAT'S UP DOC? banner, feeling like a security guard. I tried to remember what else I wasn't supposed to say to what family members. Her tiny mother whisked by without a word, close enough to let me know she'd seen me, and her squat dad shook my hand and said he'd be right back, and her cousins nodded cool hellos from across the room. The only person who stopped to talk was Jiselle, Bernadette's kid sister, a self-assured high school senior with her sights set on a career in criminal forensics. She wore Día de los Muertos skull earrings, a Dimmu Borgir T-shirt, and short shorts. She wanted to know if my classes were just as full of slackers and quitters as hers were, or if that was what was glorious about grad school, that all the fuckups were Darwined out. When I graduated, would I be presented with an ancient treasure map instead of a diploma? What was I learning about right now, this week, today? "Bones," I said. "I fucking love bones," she said, punching the air, "tell me what you know about bones!" I said that a bone's strength was directional, anchored in anticipated angles of usage; I said that although a close study of a complete skeleton would reveal a database's worth of facts specific to that deceased individual, bones were more alike from one person to another than not; I said that bones were what we carried, and at the same time, what carried us. "That is fucking amazing," said Jiselle. "I can't fucking wait. I can't fucking wait to see the world that way!" A shriveled pair of great-uncles, slurping on margaritas, evil-eyed us. Nobody in the family wanted Jiselle to study dead bodies. She was supposed to be a real doctor, like her gastroenterologist mom, or an ambitious nurse, like her PhD-pursuing sister.

It was at this moment that Dominic, the only person at the party more disliked than me, stepped in to "rescue" Jiselle. He pointed at her. "Your mother has a request," he said. She rolled her eyes but followed him—he stopped to scold her in my line of sight. Dominic had the shape of a trash bag about to burst. His face was wide, but everything on it was close together, which gave him the appearance of being in a state of constant irritation, which he was. Like Bernadette, he was a nurse who hated being a nurse. Unlike Bernadette, he didn't keep it to himself. Anytime I'd seen him at a family party, he'd gone from complaining about a terminally ill patient's whiny demands to shouting insults at a cousin's significant other to threatening to skull-fuck the peacemaking uncle who stepped in to mediate. He was the kind of man who wanted to look like he was looking for a fight.

Everybody but Bernadette blamed it on his divorce.

"He's been an angsty teenage bastard since birth," she'd said.

"Stanley is a caveman," Dominic said to Jiselle. "Stay away from cavemen."

I relocated to the bar. The only open stool was next to Bernadette's dad. When I took it, he stood up, as if he'd just remembered to feed the meter.

I examined myself in the bar mirror: it was true that I should have shaved.

Older family members left.

Dance music thumped and buzzed.

Dominic called somebody a "cocksmoker."

Bernadette and her work friends pounded shots, and instead of saying, "Cheers!" they said, "Medicine!"

Dominic said, "You don't know how to listen!"

Bernadette's parents pulled on their coats. They gave their

daughter long, proud hugs. As Bernadette watched them leave, her performance of Successful Bernadette slackened—guilt and fear wrinkled through, and pain—but as soon as she caught me staring, she straightened herself into a how-dare-you frown. She pouted over to a group of aunts and uncles.

Dominic intercepted her, flagging her down like she was a server.

No longer needing to pretend to be a nonsmoker, I went to the beer garden, a patio enclosed by weathered stone walls and scrappy old trees. Crushed leaves scraped and crinkled, scooting on the wind. A group of Bernadette's work friends swapped racist impersonations of their boss. From where I stood, they were backlit, a gallery of shit-talking shadows.

"Yo, what's your name again?" said one to me.

"Stan," said another. "His name is Stan."

"Stan the Man!" said one.

"Let me ask you something, Stan the Man," said the first one, laughing.

"Oh, leave the guy alone," said another.

"It's a personal question," said the first one.

I took a step toward them.

"What," I said.

They stopped talking.

I put out my cigarette.

Back inside, Bernadette and Dominic were yelling at each other. Spectators ringed them, friends and family alike, some grinning, some recording the fight on their phones. Dominic yelled that nurses like Bernadette were destroying the profession with their checkbox pursuit of meaningless degrees, and Bernadette yelled that it was male nurses like Dominic, with their long-standing disproportionate share of administrative positions, who had been systematically mismanaging everything for everybody for decades. Dominic did a crybaby face, miming tears. "Grow the fuck up," said Bernadette. "*Wake* the fuck up," Dominic said, "the PhD in nursing is a joke! It's a joke

degree given to any idiot willing to go into debt to pay for it!"
Bernadette's face blanched; Dominic hesitated, aware of having hurt his cousin, and of having said something that wasn't even close to being true; before he could take it back, or say something worse, I pushed in between them. Dominic smiled. "Look at this Polack," he said. "You're not family, no one has to like you. Go home and put a potato in your ass!" I kept my hands at my sides. My intention wasn't to knock him down, or even to make him think that I was going to knock him down. I only wanted to provide Bernadette with an out—I thought she might shout some final words and storm off, or walk me away from Dominic, and in doing so, walk herself away from any further escalation. But she didn't take either of those actions. The action that she took was to seize me from behind, and with bare panic in her voice, yell, "Stan, no!" as if I was the one who couldn't be counted on to restrain myself, even though restraining myself was what I'd been doing since we'd decided to get to know each other, restraining myself from thinking conflict-starting thoughts and from feeling conflict-starting feelings and from asking the set of conflict-starting questions that would lead to the conversation about why in the holy fuck we bothered to be together if most of what we did was stay out of each other's way. I stood very still while Bernadette tugged at my elbows. Her fear transferred to Dominic, who covered it with a confident laugh. "Control yourself!" screamed Bernadette. I didn't; a roof crashed down in me, burying me in darkness, burying me in demolition, and I broke out of Bernadette's grip and wrenched Dominic by the shirt and walked him through scattering onlookers and into a wall, where I held him, holding him too close for him to land punches and kicks, too close for him to work what looked like barely remembered martial arts takedowns, and although part of what I was doing was waiting for him to hit me so that I would have permission to seriously hurt him, part of what I was doing was preventing him from following through on any action that

would give me that permission. He spluttered—I was pressing on his neck. I let up. He popped me with a sloppy headbutt and I felt his nose break on my forehead. Bouncers intervened, men who weren't as big as us, but were big enough.

I was outside. I was out of breath.

I was rubbing my face hard.

I was lighting a cigarette.

Bernadette was there, shouting something, and I wasn't hearing it, and she was screaming something, and I wasn't hearing it. A local homeless man who called himself The Real Thing wobbled by on a bike, singing, his bag of collected cans rattling. He threw up a peace sign. I peace-signed him back.

Bernadette plucked the cigarette out of my mouth, turned it, and stabbed it dead on my chest.

"You make me into a terrible person!" she screamed. "I'm not a terrible person!"

I called her once a day for a week or so, and she didn't answer or call me back, and then she called me once a week for a month or so, and I didn't answer or call her back, and then we were done.

"You can do way better than Bernadette," said Torrentelli. "Not her fault, but that girl's got a lot to work through."

Barton agreed: "You were basically dating yourself. Raise your standards."

I didn't regret the breakup like I'd regretted it with Ro, and thoughts of Bernadette didn't scratch across the emptiest stretches of my day like thoughts of Ro had. I'd known there was no way we were going to last. But over the next few months, when I'd spot Bernadette sitting on the L with an open book, or poking through fruit at the grocery store, or walking Mango and Coconut by the lake, on the phone with someone, laughing, it was different—everything bunched up. I'd be cramped with an urge to talk to her. Standing there, I'd imagine the conversation: I'd say the things we'd been careful not to say, and the saying of these things would take us to where we could've been, and when we were there, we were happier, if not happy. I couldn't tell if Bernadette saw me staring at her on these occasions, but if she did, she didn't turn my way.

I decided to commit to a new simplicity. I bought a week's worth of the same shirts, jeans, slacks, and boxers. I shaved daily and kept to a monthly haircut. I returned to my boxing workout: bags, weights, cardio, cardio, weights, bags. I went to class when there was class and I went to work if there was work and I went to Huettenbar for happy hour with Torrentelli and Barton. I wanted to be a long dumb line, running straight, running blank, and for the most part, I was. In class, I wasn't; in class I was a shorter, sharper line, a line that aimed to shoot through to the insides of ideas—hypotheses and conclusions, beliefs and customs and cultures, the lost lives of vanished peoples. I was outside of any intended routine. I was someone else, someone stranger, someone brighter.

I said to myself: This someone is your reason.

This someone is the reason Bernadette wouldn't believe existed.

This someone is the reason you knew you had, the reason you felt, the reason you didn't know the shape or the size or the weight of until now.

This someone is who you want to begin to become, I said to myself.

The next step was to join a dig. To work with a team in the dirt. To be on-site, all day, screening soil for the scattered fragments of forgotten peoples—bones and ruins, splinters and bits and shards—cleaning and cataloguing, drafting reports, readying conclusions, and at the end of the day, with the team, around a fire, debating dimensions of meaning.

I applied for summer internships at competitive excavation sites, and although I came close with one, I didn't land it.

Dr. Madera, my advisor, assured me that before long, I'd be in the hole.

"Most people get really boring when they have a significant other," said Barton. "You get really boring when you're single."

I'd been explaining what could be learned from the analysis of ancient garbage.

"Play the field!" said Torrentelli. "All the fish in the sea are your oysters, and other clichés!"

Barton slid his phone to Torrentelli. It was open to a dating app I'd used. "Stan's got to change his profile picture."

Torrentelli agreed. "You look like a dad."

"He looks like he *lives* with a dad," said Barton.

I didn't change my picture. I had a drink at a downtown pub with a social media consultant and a lunch at a taqueria with a hair stylist and a dinner at a sad sports bar with a no-show and an afternoon at a neighborhood music festival with an academic assistant who revealed that she was "semi-happily married" and a night at the Lincoln Park Zoo with a line cook on cocaine, and after that, I went to a Hypocrites play at the Den with a woman named T.

Stanley Decides to Day-Trip from Prague to the Sedlec Ossuary in Kutná Hora

The space at the center of myself that wasn't me had expanded. It was nothing like an emptiness: it was full of itself.

I had stayed facedown on the couch.

The hallway and the stairwell had stayed quiet.

I shuffled off the couch and unpacked my laptop. A flickering one-bar network called CAFÉ HOUSE FREE offered access. No email from T. One from my brother, the subject line reading, "Tip #3: Fried Cheese Sandwich Right Now," and in the body, the cartoony image of a man holding a sandwich, his head exploding.

I picked up my Prague guidebook and made another go at finding the things to see and the interest to see them, but the words flattened like they'd flattened on the plane, and I slid from them into other thoughts, meaning T. Meaning T rose in me. T rose in me in a looming in-love way—her face filled me up, completely, but other faces flickered in hers somehow, as faces do in dreams—and despite my hoping otherwise, seeing T's face in me in this way again, in Prague, didn't make me wild and loose with the in-love hope of when we'd met. Instead it had me feeling handcuffed.

I opened the only other book I'd brought, *Sacred Centers: New Perspectives on North American Burial Mounds.* Dr. Madera was right; after my second year in the program, I was accepted at a summer dig—the one she co-directed, at the Cahokia Mounds State Historic Site, in Collinsville, Illinois. On the first day, Dr. Madera gave a copy of *Sacred Centers* to me and one to Golnaz. This was the book she'd worked on with her own professor-mentor, the book that had come out of *her* first dig. On the cover, a notated line drawing diagrammed the excavated interior of an archaeologically significant platform mound, the name or number of which I didn't know. This book, I felt, was more than a book. It was a gate. When I went through it I would be on the way to who I was becoming.

On the second day of the Cahokia dig, I quit.

The day after that I called the graduate school director and dropped out of the program.

I didn't answer classmates' texts, I didn't answer classmates' emails.

I didn't give the complete explanation to T.

I removed archaeology books from my nightstand and I unsubscribed from archaeology websites.

But a few months later, while packing for the flight to Prague, I'd been unable to stop myself from reaching for *Sacred Centers*. Into my bag it went. It was as if the book contained two tracks: one corroded, one clean; one shameful, one joyful. To read it was to ride both routes at once. I half-read the book to half-stop myself from seeing T. Bundles of bones buried with pottery shards and marine shells. Data on the Cahokian diet. Topographical maps of terrain through which I'd carried equipment. Hyper-specific fact-packed charts like the ones I'd intended to learn to make.

I imagined throwing the book across the room.

I threw the book across the room—it banged the wall and ruffle-fluttered to the floor. I was a baby.

I remembered: not far outside of Prague, my brother had told me, was a famous Black Death ossuary, a chapel in a church's basement done up elaborately in dead people's bones.

"Right up your creepy alley!" he'd said.

I opened the guidebook to find it. I thought about what T would say when I told her that the first thing I did when I got to Prague was leave it.

She'd say, You're a stereotype.

I'd say, And you're not.

I can commit!

You said no. You did.

I said no because you didn't mean it, she'd say. And let's speak from the I, not the you.

I'd say: I thought about it and I bought the ring and I proposed and I meant it.

Or I'd say: I may not have meant it then but I mean it now, I can mean it now.

She'd throw on her truth-face. Her truth-face was firm. It was and wasn't patient.

I'd say, Say it.

She'd say something true about our relationship.

It'd be hard to hear. I'd pretend to think about it, and then I'd say something untrue.

She'd ask a question.

I'd say something untrue.

She'd continue to truth-face me, no longer needing to speak, and in the silence I'd think of the true things that I could've said instead, that I should've said, and I'd pick one, the biggest one, and I'd imagine myself saying it. Then I'd look at T and try to say it. I'd fail. There'd be a feeling in the way, a feeling spread across me like a sealant. It wasn't anger or pride or fear or shame, but anger and pride and fear and shame were part of its compound. T would touch my arm. She'd say the true thing I'd tried to say. But instead of seeing her honesty and empathy, I'd see an actor—I'd see an actor playing Honest Empathetic Girlfriend—I'd see T's skill and talent and training, the of-this-world authenticity that she flesh-and-blooded into every role—I'd see the times I'd seen her truth-face on the stage.

This was when I'd start to swerve away from myself.

The swerving, I knew, was unsafe.

T would say, Don't leave.

I'd leave—I'd walk out of wherever we were, apartment or diner or park, bar or coffee shop, L platform, and I'd wait, waiting until my swerve away from myself had straightened out. I'd wait a little longer. I'd go back. She'd be where she'd been. She'd let me touch her arm like she'd touched mine. I'd say that who we'd been, just then, that wasn't us.

She'd say, You think you can be anybody else?

11

Stanley Recalls a Time When He Thought He Could Be Anybody Else

When I walked into the theater for our first date, T was in the lobby reading the program, chuckling to herself. We exchanged a mock-formal handshake.

She was tall and at ease and direct, playful but grounded. Her voice radiated ability—a power and a range that the moment didn't require—all of which she kept in check with practiced self-control. It was like being in the presence of an off-duty superhero.

I missed the first thing she said, an explanation of a coincidence, a personal connection to what she'd seen in the program.

"That shouldn't be surprising!" she said. "But it is."

I shook my head in a way that I hoped was worldly.

We walked to our seats. The way she moved, spoke, and grinned gave me the feeling that I should already know who she was, that if I could stop looking at how she looked at me long enough to think about it, I'd remember that I'd met her or had wanted to meet her, that we shared a friend of a friend, that we'd grown up on opposite sides of the same hometown.

None of this had come through in her profile picture, where all she'd been was beautiful.

The play was a murder mystery comedy. The seating was "immersive"—chairs had been arranged all over the set, and the audience was encouraged to change places, to catch the show from a range of angles. The actors moved through us, forcing us to switch positions. When T and I were separated, I didn't watch the play; I watched T watching. Her grin was gone. She seemed to have shifted into the insulated center of a daydream. I couldn't tell if she was completely absorbed in the play, and feeling it, or completely removed, and missing it.

Afterwards we went for tacos and beers at Big Star. We sat on the jam-packed patio, facing Damen Avenue, where the weekend mob of hipsters and bros and tourists and homeless men and women walked and biked and begged. T tied her hair back. She said that for her, the play's staging (mainly the immersive seating) invited an intellectual response, while the play's tone (mainly the actors' performances) invited an emotional response. What she appreciated, though, was how these responses were aesthetically complementary. The acknowledgment of formal artifice (how the actors made no attempt to pretend that the audience wasn't right there, sharing the stage with them) somehow *increased* the visceral pleasure of narrative immersion, of tumbling into the world of the characters. "That's not an easy thing to keep together," said T. "Everybody's got to be all-in all the time, the actors, the crew, the audience." I said that I'd seen a Hypocrites play a year or so ago, with my aunt, where they'd done a similar kind of seating—with fewer seats and more standing around—but because the play was a tragedy, not a comedy, my awareness of my fellow audience members intensified my discomfort. "I didn't like that feeling," I said. "But that feeling was part of the point."

The Big Star menu didn't include dessert.

"Tequila?" said T.

T talked about a semester she'd spent in Bali, and I talked about a world arts festival I'd attended on the South Side, again with my aunt, and we debated what it meant about a culture when its artistic traditions didn't require practitioners to slot "theater," "storytelling," "music," and "dance" into discrete categories, when what was expected was an interactive blend of many mediums.

T spoke out of performance studies and I spoke out of cultural anthropology.

We stopped at one tequila—we both had work early.

I walked her to the Damen Blue Line. She was taking the train; I was taking the bus.

"I didn't ask the get-to-know-you questions," I said. "I didn't even ask where you work."

She bopped me on the arm. "Next time."

I gave her a sincere hug.

"You don't need much to make you happy," she said, happily.

Over text we played a game of avoiding asking the get-to-know-you questions.

A week later we met at the Field Museum, where Dr. Madera had contributed to the *Ancient Americas* exhibit. We continued our conversation about art and history and representation, wandering from hall to hall, letting what we saw in the cases and read on the displays lead us to new subjects.

On the steps outside, she said, "We just gave each other a guided tour."

"We're professionals," I said.

We sat. Summer camp kids in bright T-shirts swarmed the steps, shouting and squealing, running and shoving. The street was lined with idling buses. Blinding wedges of sunlight erased the surfaces of skyscrapers.

T put her hand on mine.

"Do it," she said.

I kissed her.

She was an actor: I watched her rehearsals. I was a graduate student: she read my research. We met each other's friends and we ate at each other's favorite restaurants and we attended each other's social gatherings, and although we didn't directly ask where we were from and what we did for work, the answers jumped up on their own. T was from a far north suburb, I was from a far south suburb; our parents had separated; she was a volunteer grant-writer for an arts education nonprofit, and a server at a brewpub, and a hostess-in-training at an upscale Mexican restaurant, and the coordinator of a theater summer camp for gifted grade schoolers.

I worked construction for subcontractors and I went to class.

"You're smart," she said. "You know to keep it simple."

Keep it simple, I said to myself.

The first night that I spent at T's place on purpose, I brought a change of clothes. In the morning, while she watched from bed, I stepped into a pair of sweatpants and a hooded sweatshirt. They were stretched and faded, worn and frayed. She hubba-hubbaed. I flexed. She sat up, out of the sheets, naked, and raised her hand like we were in a classroom. She couldn't stop it: wherever she was, whatever she did, she supercharged her personal space with an aura of casual celebrity. This was the source of what I'd felt when we met, the feeling that I ought to know her. More than once a week, a stranger would go out of his or her way to ask her if she'd ever been told that she looked like a certain actor, comedian, musician, model, athlete. I'd seen it happen on the street and at parties, in grocery stores and at museums, on the L and at red lights. In bed, with her hand raised, she looked like she was in the intro to a music video, like her world was about to go fantastical with song and light. She waved her hand harder. I called on her. She asked if I'd ever been told that I looked like a character from a high school football movie. "The Quarterback," I said. "No, the Center," she said, dropping her voice to imitate a doofy jock, "the Quarterback's Dumb Best Friend." I looked at the mirror nailed to the back of her door: she was right. That week I stopped shaving and I skipped the haircut. She touched my sprouting cheek. "Supercop on the Case," she said. I returned to shaving. As my hair got longer, but not long, she compared me to other types, in the voices of those types—"Supercop on the Case, in a Comedy," "Frustrated FBI Agent," "Ethically Conflicted Hit Man"—but when I wore the shirts and slacks and jeans she gave me, and the sweaters her abuela gave me, and the shoes her pops gave me, and the most rugged cologne that the man at the Nordstrom's could find, she started to say that I looked like myself.

"Tell me what that means."

She thought about it. "You look like you feel like yourself."

I said that everything was tight.

She tapped my butt. "That's because it fits."

12

Stanley Day-Trips to the Sedlec Ossuary in Kutná Hora

A train took me to Kutná Hora in two hours, rattling around green mountains and rivers. Alone in the car, I read about the layers of Cahokian burial mounds that'd been stuffed with the whole skeletons of important Cahokians. The main thing we know about important Cahokians, Dr. Madera liked to say, was that they were important. The train whumped and shuddered like a school bus. I closed the book. I began to feel, with my body, that I was in a foreign country, in the realm of customs and rules I didn't know but was subject to, and that it was important to admit to this, to be attentive to my ignorance. At the station I stepped off and followed a handful of fellow tourists from other cars into the road.

A sign read FIFTEEN MINUTE WALK THIS WAY.

In a scattered group we passed a shut-down factory, a row of saggy homes, a garage, a bar, a garage-like bar. Smoking locals stared from open doors, their disinterest fierce.

Two men at the front of our group, annoyed, traded camera lenses.

Three women shared a bag of apple slices.

A boy in a soccer jersey snapped practice pictures of his grandpa.

The church appeared at the top of a tombstone-cluttered hill, the hump of earth like some giant's sunken severed head, the slanted stones the ruins of her crown. This was where an abbot brought a jar of dirt he'd collected from the hill where Christ was killed, I'd read, where he spread it, where the rich outbid one another to be buried. A breeze flickered by, stinking of spilled chemicals. The grandpa pretended he'd farted. The boy, wanting to believe him, laughed.

We entered the church. We bought tickets at the gift-shoppy front desk. We headed down the steps and were there.

The space was stone-chambered and shadowy, lit like a low-budget set. Bones lined the ceiling's vaulted contours. Bones ran the walls in bristling banners. Bones stood as sculptures, throne-sized, assembled into chalices and holy crosses and a coat of arms. Although these arrangements of skulls and ribs and pelvises and vertebrae and femurs and humeri were unintended by the body, they had the look of a series of solved puzzles. The centerpiece was a chandelier. It hung in a cake-like tapering heap. It was precisely like and unlike a chandelier, its levels ornate, various, each design yet another clever use of the body's very smallest bones. Pillars fenced it in. On the pillars sat painted wooden cherubs, and on their fat laps, skulls.

PLEASE RESPECT THIS SACRED PLACE, warned the signs.

An excited young man reviewed the pictures he'd taken with his phone, and a middle-aged woman shook her head at the artist's wall-mounted signature-in-fingerbones, and an attractive woman, my age, argued with her attractive companion, a man twice my age, in a language I couldn't identify. These reactions I understood. Whatever blend they were of awe and revulsion and humor and fear, they were the product of considering the how and the why of the existence of this site, the how and the why explained in the church's free pamphlet, the basement's many placards, and my guidebook: the thousands of fifteenth-century plague victims mass-buried in the church-yard's sacred soil; the lone sixteenth-century monk, half-blind, half-mad, who'd exhumed and rearranged the victims' bones into shrine-like pyramids; and the nineteenth-century nobleman who'd commissioned a professional artist to continue the monk's work, to make what was left of the dead into an offering to themselves.

I saw the others seeing some or all of this. I saw myself seeing them seeing this. I admit: it was satisfying.

I felt grateful to my brother.

On my way out I stumbled on the stairs, not enough to make me fall but enough to make me turkey-flap my arms. Someone I didn't see tittered.

I walked to the tracks alone. A middle-aged man sat on a bench under the station's awning, reading a newspaper. It was the made-up man from the airport.

He now wore sparkly earrings. His makeup had been reapplied. When I passed him, he smelled like prom.

The attractive couple who'd been going at it in the ossuary arrived, still ticked at each other. They lit the last two cigarettes in their pack. The man tossed the pack onto the rails, acting like he didn't know that this would infuriate the woman. She blew a fuck-you of smoke into his face. He smiled.

The made-up man rose. He paced the platform, fake-reading, and came to a gradual stop in a position from which he could be sure that I'd see the front page. It featured a black-and-white photo of me and him at the airport, the moment when I took the key. The transaction looked criminal: my scowl nervous, his smile derisive.

I stayed where I was. He stayed where he was.

When the train could be heard down the track, grinding and hissing, he lowered the newspaper, "saw" me, and pretended to be startled. Then concerned. Then concerned about me seeing his concern.

He approached me like I might hurt myself.

I put the attractive couple between us, boarded, and picked an empty car.

We pulled away from the station. I watched the door's dirty window.

At the next stop a grim dad and his two grim daughters shuffled in and sat across from me. They unwrapped ham sandwiches and ate.

One of the girls stared at me, mustard on her teeth.

By early afternoon the train had returned to Prague. I walked from the station to the apartment, stopping at a corner store for pop, beer, and snacks. The clerk noted but did not acknowledge my entrance. I appreciated this: it reminded me that I was in a city. Club music played. The things I wanted weren't where I thought they'd be and looked nothing like I expected them to look. Bags of chips by jars of fish, cases of cola on crates of bleach. I imagined telling this to T. She liked to retell my stories to her friends, stories she wasn't in or hadn't witnessed. She'd perform them with theatrical intensity, enriching and estranging the facts with voices and gestures, with wry philosophical asides. Her friends, also actors, would cheer with delight. One of them would buy me a drink I didn't want. T would punctuate her performance with happy glances in my direction, glances that were part of the performance. I'd stay silent. All of this fuss over one of my stories was to some extent an honor, I felt that, but the way it center-staged me without my participation made me uneasy, and the way T took liberties with the source material—me, and my way of telling my stories—set us up for disagreement.

Right, she'd say, because you tell *our* stories so correctly. Correctly Stanley, that's what they call you. Correct me, Correctly Stanley! I'm an error!

I'm not saying you're incorrect. I'm saying you're not *correct*.

And I'm not saying you can't admit when you're wrong. I'm saying you can't admit when you're not *right*. I'm also not saying you're a dickhead, I'm saying you're Head Dick.

I laughed out loud. The clerk, ringing up my purchases, was unaffected. He looked like he laughed just once a week when he fell off a bar stool. The fact that I didn't matter to him any more or less than anyone else made me feel almost as good as I'd felt in the ossuary. The columns of cigarettes behind him did not batter down the door to my addiction. He handed back my change. I said, "Děkuji."

He looked up from his phone. "Prosím," he said, as though it broke a superstition not to.

When I got back to the apartment the pesticidal stench had dissipated. I put the drinks in the fridge and went to the couch with a can of pop. The couch squeaked.

I opened my laptop. The background on my desktop had changed.

It had been a color picture I'd taken of a mound at Cahokia. It was now a black-and-white picture of me, framed through a filthy window. I was seated, glaring—it was from the train I'd just been on. It took me a moment to realize that my glare was directed at the grim girl, who wasn't in the shot. I looked like I was contemplating committing a criminal act.

My brother had predicted less intrusiveness from Uncle Lech and the artists. My father, more.

To me it didn't matter: my strategy was set.

I changed the background back. I checked my sent-box. I checked my in-box. Manny had written me:

Ciao Stanley:
     I will be arriving at 16:15, di Firenze, and will be in molto need of a recommendation for a ristorante that will disappoint me but slightly. Va bene? I leave in one hour, and while I am eager to enjoy the opportunities of Golden Praha, and to reconvene with T, already I miss Il Bel Paese, where all things are più semplici.
     A presto,
     Manny.

Manny was T's best friend from high school. They'd stayed close. Although I'd only seen him a few times, he had given me many rotten moments to remember him by. Last winter he flew from Berlin to Chicago for the holidays. T and I took him and his companion, Inna, out bowling. To make conversation, to try like T had wanted me to try, I'd asked Manny where he'd been traveling lately. He'd said, like he was wearing a cape, "Everywhere and nowhere." It made me want to punch him in the glasses.

Stanley Recalls the Last Time He Talked to Manny

"Everywhere and nowhere," he said.

I finished my beer. Pins cracked across the lanes.

He picked up his bowling ball, a kid's model labeled OUTTA THIS WORLD. "But do not get the idea that I am a 'traveler,' Stanley, or a 'tourist,' or a 'volunteer,' or any other synonym for 'the unambitious.'"

He bowled the ball between his legs and struck the head pin. Only five fell.

T, sitting next to Inna on the other side of the console, grinned at me. Her grin hit gorgeous, grateful, and pitying—it seemed lifted straight from the face of some famous sitcom character—and it made me angry, which made me sad.

Stanley Naps

No email from T.

I said to myself: It would be worse to hear from her than to not hear from her.

Myself said: You don't believe you.

I do and I don't.

You don't.

I closed my laptop and lay down on the couch. The cushions had an unplaceable smell.

I dropped hard into a dream I wouldn't remember.

Stanley Remembers the Dream

I was napping on a couch in a room in which every surface was a couch.

An invisible lid, very wide and thick and heavy, slammed closed on me repeatedly.

I had the sense that the lid was doing this without actually opening.

I had the sense that I was inside the space at the center of myself that wasn't me.

I had the sense that being inside the space at the center of myself that wasn't me should be providing me with helpful information, but wasn't.

The lid slammed and slammed and slammed without a sound.

I had the sense that there should have been an echo.

Stanley Wakes Up as Manny Arrives

The door buzzer squawked.

I pulled myself to my feet. I buzzed Manny in, unlocked and opened the door, and stepped back.

The door downstairs whomped shut. The staircase crackled and wheezed like it was more than one Manny coming to stay the night, more than one Manny who'd nobly endure me until T's arrival tomorrow afternoon. He paused in what sounded like the middle of each flight. In these silences I imagined him cataloguing architectural flaws, or constructing condescending questions, or converting the things that T had told him about recent events in my life into a sequence of backhanded compliments, or planning the timing of the ending of a story that was meant to suggest to the women he was interested in that his pseudo-intellectual elitism was the front to a sensibility so tender, so secretly compassionate, and so unfairly unrecognized that he had earned the right to a gentle hand job from the world.

He reached my floor, and paused. He walked the hall to just before my doorway, and paused. He appeared.

Manny was skinny but broad-shouldered somehow, tanned, his eyes so wide he'd look bewildered if it wasn't for how he never hid his sizing-up of everything and everyone he saw. His glasses and watch were hip. He wore a white T-shirt and dark slacks. The slacks were pressed.

"I have been deceived," he declared.

I'd forgotten how deep his voice landed. His arms, which I'd never seen, were matted in sweaty hair.

"The location is exceptional. The apartment is not."

He walked past me and into the kitchen, where he opened and closed every drawer. In the bathroom he pushed aside the shower curtain to examine the tub, and in the bedroom he shoved aside my luggage to peek under the bed, and in the living room he sat. The couch tooted.

I closed and locked the door.

He picked up both of my books, one from the coffee table and one from the floor.

I went to the fridge for another pop.

He read out loud from my guidebook: "'Unlike many of their neighbors, the citizens of this small, landlocked country have rarely resisted as armies marched across their borders, often choosing to fight with words instead of weapons.'" He smirked. "Not one Czech in all of Prague would approve of that passage."

"You don't know that," I said.

He flipped to the phrases in the back. "Ne," he said. "Promiňte."

He shut the book and frowned at the ceiling.

"Dobrý den!" he said, conducting with his hands. "Prosím! Nashledanou!"

His accent sounded right to me, but what did I know.

"Stanley," he said. "This is merely your first day in Praha?"

I said it merely was.

"Stanley," he said. "T was mysterious. T is seldom mysterious. How did you come to occupy this apartment?"

Stanley Recounts His Aunt Abbey's Birthday Party

Back in July I went to my aunt Abbey's birthday grill-out at her and Uncle Lech's house in Rogers Park. Her birthday was one of the three times a year that my dad's side of the family got together, minus Busia, who refused to set foot in the city—my dad drove up from Joliet, my brother took the L from Lakeview, and I rode the bus from Lincoln Square. T had been invited. One reason she didn't come was that she was tied up with a play, the final run before their trip to Europe. The show she starred in, *Black and White and Dead All Over*, had been accepted to a big-name festival in Prague. When they'd found out mid-rehearsal, she said, they'd stripped to their underwear and run in screaming circles.

The other reason T didn't come was that she'd moved out of our apartment and into the apartment of several of her castmates. We weren't broken up but we were on a break. I'd proposed and she'd said no.

The party was the day after celebrations for the Fourth, and a fat heat sat on the city. The lake-wind way up in Rogers Park brought relief to the neighborhood. As I walked from the bus stop, cool gusts kicked blown bottle rockets and plastic cups around the alleys. I practiced looking like I felt okay.

Their house was the only crummy one on the block, a gloomy two-flat propped between a pair of tidy renovated greystones. I bumped open the gate—a tangle of grotesque wooden dolls, hung where bells might be expected, clattered and clapped, their little heads looking dumbstruck. Aunt Abbey leaned out a window near the end of the house, from the kitchen. Her silver-streaked hair was done up in a bun and her face and neck were flushed from the kitchen's heat. She wore a simple sundress she'd designed and sewn herself. In it, she looked more like my mom than my dad, despite the fact that my dad was her brother. Her face smiled without smiling. Even if she weren't my only aunt, she'd be my favorite.

I gave her a bottle of Chopin and told her to hide it better than she'd hid it last year.

She spoke into the cap like it was a microphone: "Every hiding place I know was his first."

Then she fumbled the bottle—I caught it by the neck before it hit the concrete.

"Drinking already," I said, handing her the bottle again.

She pulled back into the kitchen. "If only!"

My dad and my brother were in the backyard, beers in hand and playing bags. I hadn't seen my brother since May, when I'd quit the dig at Cahokia.

"Holy smokes," he said, "who invited the beard?"

"You play winner," said my dad.

My brother tickled my beard and in a baby voice said, "Wook whose gwoing up! Stanwee! Stanwee's a *bwig* boy!"

I asked if anyone was low. My brother presented his cup. I took it to the keg by the warped sunporch, plucked my own off the cup-stack, and filled them. The backyard was small, crowded with planter boxes and piles of garbage pickings. We played bags in the only available open lane of weedy grass. The garage—massive, mounded in creeping vines and suckers— was our uncle's workshop. We'd never entered it. Displayed throughout the yard were its poisoned fruits, the "seasonal exhibit": on that day, life-sized 2-D flats of men and women, sawed in such a way as to make them look like they were emerging from and disappearing into the garden, the gutters, the patio's ruptured concrete, the fence's slats. They'd been painted in a kind of highly stylized grayscale, with suits and ties and dresses and hats, and were closer to silhouettes than not. It was like we'd walked into a film-noir-themed shooting range.

I tried to remember what the summer exhibit had been the year before and couldn't.

Next to the keg was the card table laden with platters of pierogi, gołabki, potato pancakes, and beet salad, and next to that, the sausage table, a multi-plattered abundance of grilled, roasted, and boiled kiełbasa, smoked and fresh, ringed by a sliced assortment of cold sausages and cheeses and pickles, and bread.

I made a plate and carried it between the two cups. While I walked I forgot to remember that we weren't supposed to enjoy anything about being there.

My dad landed one bag on the board. He missed with the rest.

My brother hit two in the hole.

"I've seen crazier comebacks," said my brother.

My dad helped himself to the food I offered. As he ate he made angry affirmative noises. There was a bandage on his neck.

He noticed my new beard but said nothing.

I asked if the artists were in the garage or what.

"Can't you hear it?" said my brother, baffled.

I stopped chewing.

"You can't?" said my dad. "How? Tell me how, so I can't too."

Something in the garage sounded like a hog. Then it sounded like a bunch of hogs, and then not at all like hogs but like many dire men saying things as deeply as they could. And maybe a saxophone.

"They must be having Mass," said my brother.

My dad grunted. "If they are they're eating the priest."

I studied the garage. Between vines twinkled a magnificent stained-glass window. Stained glass was how Uncle Lech made an obscenity of money, our dad had claimed, but it sure wasn't what we ever saw him making. When we visited for Christmas Eves, Easters, and Aunt Abbey's birthdays, he was perpetually mid-project with his commune of who we took to be his fellow recently expatriated foreign artists, probably Poles like him, and like him, certifiable. They lived on and off in the garage. They wandered through the yard and the house, performing.

Stanley Recalls the Artist with the Drawings on His Face

He'd pretend he couldn't see you. If you met him in a hallway, he'd bump you gently until you moved. He was built like a washing machine. The drawings on his face, different every time, imitated patriotic tattoos and always depicted a bald eagle taloning his nose. Sometimes the bald eagle was obese. One time it had boobs. Its boobs dripped drops of milk that turned into eggs that hatched American flags.

Stanley Recalls the Artist with the Laugh

He'd dress like different white American stereotypes—a hipster, a hick, a yuppie, a dude-bro—and as soon as you came close enough to hear him, he'd laugh. His laughter, which wasn't "in character," was always the same: disbelieving. If you looked at him he stopped. If you looked away he started up again.

Stanley Recalls the Artist Who Pretended to Be Homeless

He'd set up in the house. With the help of makeup and latex, his face took on different devastated textures, from a sallow tubercular glow to a ripped-up dryness to a matrix of shining open sores. He'd speak frustrated nonsense words and nest in cardboard boxes by the bathroom door or under the dining room table, shaking a cup or holding a sign.

Stanley Recalls the Artist Who Pretended to Be Asleep, Comatose, or Dead

She'd be sprawled facedown in a hallway, dressed as a minimum-wage employee, often a fast-food worker. You'd step over her. Later she'd turn up in a more challenging place: on top of a bookshelf, under a rug.

Stanley Recalls the Artist with the Easel

He or she wore an American-flag bandanna on his or her face, a patriotic baseball hat, and a smock that was a frumpy suit blazer put on the wrong way, back to front. When you sat to eat, he or she would set up behind you with an easel. If you shifted, he or she would shift to stay at your back. The quick sketch he or she made in charcoal was of an artist sketching you from behind, except the artist in the sketch wasn't the artist, it was you.

Stanley Reflects on Uncle Lech's Art

If you came to Uncle Lech's you were the audience for and subject of an art project, one that hit the intersection of performance art, conceptual art, and the plastic arts. Although the artists appeared to pursue individual projects, Uncle Lech regularly turned their energies toward the completion of more ambitious group projects, phases of which we sometimes witnessed.

My brother loved it. It made him laugh. He loved to hear his own grand laugh. After writing computer code all day for his incompetent boss's incompetent bosses, he said, he toggled his brain to OFF, and what was better for the entertainment of an OFF brain than art made out of practical jokes?

My father despised it. He despised Uncle Lech, his sister's marriage to Uncle Lech, and the artists, who he never called artists, only "the creeps." Their art wasn't art, he'd say, it wasn't even jokes, it was tricks, and every one of them was on whoever the hell happened to be nearby.

Aunt Abbey, when asked, invoked aesthetic categories: "There is art that engages, and art that estranges. And there is art that engages-estranges, in equal measure, from beginning to end."

I was undecided.

"You mean 'uninformed,'" T would say, whenever it came up.

I had to admit that I'd never seen his work exhibited.

Before we met, T had encountered my uncle and his work at a pop-up gallery in Wicker Park. The evening's featured artists were either established heavyweights or talked-about up-and-comers. T's friend Sarah-Joseph, a talked-about up-and-comer, was exhibiting a sequence of cosmologically themed sculptures, which T had modeled for. The sculptures had scored positive write-ups in important art magazines, no small feat, but the evening's magnetic center was my uncle's installation *Country-Western Country*. For this project, he and his artists had formed a fake country-western band (the Achy-Breakies), played semi-parodic songs that alternately enchanted, confused, and enraged the audiences at country-western bars in downstate Illinois, Chicagoland, and Chicago (most notably at Carol's, in Uptown), and documented the experience with photos and audio and video, with performance reviews and news articles, with cracked instruments and half-shattered beer bottles and blood-smudged bar napkins. This exhibit was the only one to claim its own entire room in the gallery.

T understood what my uncle was up to with his art, and why it had a big draw, but she couldn't support his approach.

"If your uncle's subject is 'America,'" she said, "it's not an America that most Americans live in, with his ten white men per one white woman and all of them from fucking Poland."

"'America' isn't his subject," I said. "His subject is 'This Is How I Imagine America.'"

"'This Is How I Imagine America' is the subject of 'America.'"

I conceded that this was a good point.

"But that's not *his* point," she said. "His point is that he doesn't care how his art affects the people that it exploits. When I was younger, I thought an attitude like that was absolutely essential, was how you made real work. Now I know it's just convenient."

Near the end of the night Sarah-Joseph introduced T to my uncle. They met in the *Country-Western Country* room, every wall dense with labeled artifacts.

My uncle looked at T like she was a shelf full of art supplies.

"Your model," he said, addressing Sarah-Joseph.

Sarah-Joseph gave T a squeeze. "Couldn't have done it without her."

"Oh, cut it out," said T. "The artist does the work."

My uncle agreed. "The model is nothing."

Sarah-Joseph laughed.

My uncle pantomimed a scene with his hands. "Here is the artist; here is the nothing. The artist is going to the nothing, is saying: I see? Something? I see? The nothing is doing nothing. The nothing is doing the nothing in the nowhere, with the no one and the no time. Reality. Then the artist: Am I seeing? Am I seeing now? Yes—in the nothing, the artist is seeing the model. Do you understand? The artist is making the model where there is no model. Always. Always the artist is making the art where there is no art."

"Nope," said Sarah-Joseph. "That's not how it works for me. There's communion between artist and subject, between concept and medium. There's reciprocity. There's never a 'nothing' that I turn into a 'something.'"

My uncle's response was to direct them to three large-format photos taken during the Achy-Breakies' show at Carol's. The first was a wide shot of the stage. Every member of the band was playing, except the bassist, a square man who sat on the floor in a state of shame, hiding his face in his cowboy hat. In the second, my uncle, the lead singer, was reaching somewhat romantically toward a lone woman at the front of the crowd, her back to the lens. The final photo was a profile of this woman at what appeared to be the same moment—she seemed to be suffering from a terrible emotional shock, T said, like she was being electrocuted by grief.

"Your model," said T.

My uncle motioned, with a ceremonial sweep, to the spread of art on each wall. "My model—my model—my model—my model."

Sarah-Joseph said, "How did you 'see' her, how did you 'make' her?"

He explained that this woman was the shamed bassist's sister. Their mother had recently died in a "very preventable accident." The woman looked the way she did because my uncle had been singing a version of "America the Beautiful" in which he had added lyrics that unambiguously examined her difficult relationship with her deceased mother.

"Many confidential details," said my uncle.

Sarah-Joseph was taken aback. "Confidential details you heard from her brother?"

My uncle said, "Have you heard what I have said? 'There is no hearing, there is only seeing.'"

"Never mind, I get it now," said Sarah-Joseph. "You don't want to see people as people."

My uncle didn't understand, or pretended not to understand, what this statement meant.

Sarah-Joseph ran him through a theory of ethics in art.

An item caught T's eye. She walked up to what looked like a real article from a real community newspaper, next to the trio of photos. It detailed a domestic disturbance in which a woman had pushed her brother down a flight of stairs. The man had been partially paralyzed, with several broken vertebrae, and the woman had been arrested, with no bail. Police determined that they were both undocumented immigrants from Poland. Deportation was likely.

This was when T realized that with the exception of my uncle, none of the artists depicted in the multimedia installation—the band members, the roadies, the groupies, the manager—were in attendance at the opening.

At that moment, the series curator strolled in, eating a large piece of cake. With her mouth full, she gestured for my uncle to follow her.

My uncle nodded to Sarah-Joseph, who was nearing the end of her explanation. He said, "I am excused."

24

Stanley Receives an Envelope

"Stop," said Manny, interrupting me.

He perked up like he'd heard a noise. He was sitting at the kitchen table with my guidebook.

I'd been answering his question—how I "came to occupy this apartment"—and he'd been interrupting with a series of leading questions—"Can I correctly assume that your uncle has a lucrative, legitimate, art-related day job?" and "Surely, in an art community as limited as Chicago's, T would have encountered your uncle?" and "Allow me to guess: a supposed 'tragedy' befell the bassist and the bassist's sister?"

The purpose of these interruptions was for Manny to demonstrate that he was an expert in the subject of my uncle and the artists, that thanks to T, his best friend, he knew as much about them as I did, if not more.

In this instance, however, Manny's interruption was an observation.

Then I saw it, also: a large gray envelope had slid under the door and into the apartment.

If there'd been footsteps, I hadn't heard them.

Manny shushed me, even though I wasn't speaking. He rose from his chair. He approached the envelope in an I'm-the-adult-here way.

I tore open a bag of chips.

Manny picked up the envelope. I could see but not read its label.

"'Preview of *The Made-Up Man*,'" read Manny.

He flipped it over, then back.

I didn't want him to open it, and I didn't want him to know that I didn't want him to open it. But most of all, I didn't want to care one way or the other.

"In this apartment," he decided, "I, too, am a guest."

He unsealed the envelope and withdrew a sheaf of photos.

The first one, he showed off: an impressively Photoshopped mug shot of me. I looked a very long way from repentance. The source photo had been plucked from social media, one of many shots in which I wasn't smiling. To conform to the mug-shot genre, I'd been digitally edited into holding a placard, but instead of displaying booking information, it displayed a sentence:

YOUR "LIFE" IS IN DANGER

Manny turned to the next photo. He shook his head, amused, and presented another mug shot, this one a highly textured silhouette of a woman. Her features had been mapped over with a chalky black void. It was as if she was a woman-shaped wound sliced into space-time. The placard:

TRUST "NO ONE"

This silhouette, I could tell, belonged to T.

Manny could tell too.

"These are quite 'meaningful' in their 'emphasis,'" he said.

When he flipped to the third photo, he froze. What he saw he didn't like. His face ticked from embarrassment to irritation, from surprise to confirmation. He shuffled through the rest, three or four more, not revealing those either, then tucked them back into the envelope.

I didn't need to see the third photo to know that it was of him.

He dropped the envelope onto the table, casually, and sat down. To show that he'd regained his composure—to suggest that he'd never lost it—he sighed.

He sighed again.

He said, "You have yet to tell me the manner in which your uncle offered this job to you."

"You keep interrupting me," I said.

"It is to be expected that you misconstrue my questions as 'interruptions.' 'Interruption' is the word that a person such as yourself, in a scenario such as this one, would turn to for deflective comfort. No—my questions are not 'interruptions.'"

He waited for me to ask him what his questions were.

I didn't.

He said, "They are investigations."

25

Stanley Recalls His Conversation with His Brother at His Aunt Abbey's Birthday Party

"You're up," said my dad, giving me a bag.

Along the edges of his bandage the skin of his neck rose, purple-red and puffy. He acted like he didn't see me notice, like he lacked an injury, a story about the origin of the injury, or a neck.

My brother and I played. Every bag I tossed scored—they slapped the board or punched the hole or bumped hangers in. I don't know how I did so well. I was thinking too much to be in any Zen-like zone.

My brother started up with the goofy voices:

"Where you get your HGH?"

"Those bags corked?"

I sank three holers.

"They let you play in the unemployment line?"

My dad drank his beer fast and stared into the simmering haze of neighbors' yards. In the nearest, a boy stared back, pressed against a fence, his hands tight on the handle of a wagon full of toys. He wore a monster mask.

I asked my dad how was work, how was Joliet.

"Work is work. Joliet is Joliet."

He went inside to pee.

My brother said, "Mom might 'stay' in Europe."

Every summer our mom flew abroad and thought out loud

about never coming back. During the school year she taught French and Russian at College of DuPage, a position she annually decided she'd be an idiot to leave.

"Before she left, they were hanging out again," he said.

He batted his eyebrows and made a smoochy-face.

I said nothing.

We went to the keg. He gave the back of my head a brotherly pat. Once a week he talked on the phone with our mom no matter what, and no matter what on Sundays he took our dad out to lunch. Bolts of guilt torqued in my chest. I asked what had happened to our dad's neck. My brother said he'd claimed it'd been a work accident. We agreed that this was a lie. Last summer, a growth the size of a screw had been removed from his face. We only knew about it because the before and after were right there, public. If asked, our dad had said, "It's nothing," and if pressed, he'd found some silently threatening way to say: Back off. Whenever our dad had a health problem, and avoided discussion of it, our mom liked to say that his behavior was because of his belief that talking about a bad thing he'd dealt with would bring that bad thing back worse. He'd never admit it, she insisted, but this was a family trait. Straight down the line from Busia.

"Don't think the both of *you* don't have it," she'd say to me and my brother. "You do. It's just it's less debilitating."

My brother asked me if I'd found full-time work. I hadn't. I'd been working whenever I was needed for our dad's friend Niko, a contractor he used to use, loading and unloading, doing demolition, hauling bags of the things I'd smashed into trash containers the size of trailer homes. I showed off my fingernails: each housed a mini-sickle of grime.

"Data entry," said my brother. "Every day we're hiring. Next thing you know you'll be manager. Then managing the managers! Then who knows, on to Operations. All you need to be is competent."

We ate more sausage. The weselna was best, we agreed, but only because there was no warsawska.

"The beard looks magical," he said. "I didn't think you had it in you."

It wasn't the first time I'd grown a beard, but it was the first time I'd kept one for longer than a month.

"I look like a young Dziadzia," I said.

"You look like a young Busia with a young Dziadzia's beard."

I cupped my chin and started to speak but stopped. My brother was right.

Our Busia had lived a very long bad life.

"Look," said my brother, touching my shoulder, "either you're not yourself, or you're a new yourself I'm not used to yet."

On his face had appeared the encouraging smile that signaled his receptivity to whatever response you were up to making, be it a subject-changing joke, an irritated dismissal, an obvious lie, or the warm-up to a heart-to-heart. The smile was hopeful. You could see your best self in it. My brother seemed content to wait for the day that I chose to make him my confidant, to give him permission to help me crack the hard case that I had shut myself inside. His faith in me made me feel young and dumb.

I'd said to T that who he thought I was wasn't who I was, mostly.

She'd said: "When's the last time *you* called *him*?"

The handful of times that the three of us had gone for a drink together, T and my brother had enjoyed each other's company, an enjoyment heightened by playful disbelief—for my brother, that T was my girlfriend, for T, that my brother was my brother.

She's so smart and beautiful!

He's so friendly!

It might not add up that this sort of banter would make

me feel good about who I was, or who was in my life. But it did.

"Everything cool?" said my brother.

This was when I should have told him that T had moved out.

"Is it the dig?" he said.

When I'd quit the Cahokia dig in May, I was stranded in Collinsville—I'd carpooled down with Dr. Madera and Golnaz. I called my brother for a lift back to Chicago. Otherwise I wouldn't have told him.

"Only the stupid can be happy," I said, quoting Busia.

He did her hobgoblin voice: "Life is brutal and full of traps."

26

Stanley Remembers the Final Family Dinner with Busia

Last June, days before Busia died, our dad hosted her and my brother and me for dinner, which he hadn't done since the holidays. My brother picked me up after work and we stopped-and-started through the rush-hour crawl to our dad's condo down in Joliet, in the sapling-lined complex he'd built, one of dozens of new developments springing up on old farmland every year. "Country Lane," they'd called it.

Busia was sitting at the head of the table when we walked in, critically looking on as our dad poured a can of beer into a glass for her. She was a shaved-down scrap of a woman, cut by personal and historical struggle to a state of existential indivisibility. Whatever weapon you hit her with would break. She was from Warsaw.

The only weakness she admitted to was her breathing: stuttered, gulping. It enraged her.

She'd taken to saying, "The breathing will kill me."

This acknowledgment of her condition was unlike her.

My brother kissed her on the cheek, and I kissed her on the cheek, and we sat at either side of her. She studied us, one at a time. Her face was a wall at the end of a tunnel.

Our dad set the table. He smelled like he'd been smoking cigarettes in his sleep. Last I saw him, he'd still been quit.

"This is no home," said Busia.

The condo had a new-construction echo—nothing on the walls, not much furniture. Our dad preferred the on-the-market look.

"Dinner," said our dad, popping containers of take-out Polish, spooning pierogi, cutlets, and kapusta onto Busia's plate. "It's from Old Europe Inn. You like it. We were there."

She said something in Polish.

"Eat," said our dad.

She didn't.

"Eat," said our dad to me and my brother.

We served ourselves and ate.

Our dad sat at the other end of the table, his plate empty. Busia watched him. She was a riddle, but the answer was always the same: no.

"I went on a date with a Polish girl," said my brother.

Our dad's work cell phone rang. When he pulled it out of his hip holster to see who was calling, Busia gestured for the paper take-out bag. My brother pushed it to her. She picked up her plate and turned it upside down over the bag, the food plopping and splatting.

"We can get you something else, if you want?" said my brother.

She folded the bag shut.

"For fuck's sake, it was a fucking work call," shouted our dad. "I have to work, Ma. I have to work to keep you alive."

Busia said, "Not my circus, not my monkeys."

Our dad snatched her plate and the paper bag and stomped out of the room and into the kitchen. He smashed a smashable object.

My brother hurried into the kitchen.

There was another smash.

Busia sniffed at her beer.

I tried to think of something to say to her. Although I didn't like who she was, how she treated her family, or the fact that we were related, I respected her in a way that was similar to how I respected certain despicable MMA fighters, back when I used to watch the tournaments—the same qualities that made those three or four fighters despicable people, it seemed, made them extraordinary athletes, and it felt false to hate them for the reasons that made me love watching them.

Busia rolled a fist against her chest. Her breaths stretched and wavered, slowly. She was more pale than usual, which only made her seem more dangerous. I knew better than to ask small-talky questions about how she was feeling and what she'd been up to, or genuine questions about her childhood, what it was like to immigrate, and why she'd never gone back to visit Warsaw, not even once.

In my imagination, Warsaw was a block of leveled walls and buildings, a blasted ring of rubble. Noble broken things were there. But everyone who guarded them was Busia.

I said, "If you don't want to eat, you don't have to eat."

She tilted her head, her old poker-tell for imminent violence. Then she pointed straight up, to indicate the kitchen behind her. "They are bad. But you, you are worse."

I laughed. "It's because I'm like you."

"No," she said. "It is because you do not know you are an idiot."

27

Stanley Continues to Recount Aunt Abbey's Birthday Party

My brother said, "This might be an unforgivable thing to say, but I kind of hoped it'd be easier on Dad now that Busia's gone."

I nodded. "It isn't."

We clunked our cups together in salute to Busia. We wanted to miss her, which was something like missing her.

Our dad returned, hot-faced with fury. He'd been yelling. "The bastard's hiding in the bathroom," he said. "When you have to piss, piss on him."

I had to piss. The back door led right into the kitchen, which was so crammed with antique cooking utensils and decorative nonfunctional pottery and half-completed acrylic-splashed canvases that the effect was of a space in which it was hard to tell what was meant to be art and what wasn't, which was the state of every room and hallway in the house, which Aunt Abbey said was the point of the art that mattered the most: to create the sort of space we used to see everywhere we went but had been taught by time and economics to un-see.

"We need help re-seeing," she'd say, "re-seeing everything. Starting with the self."

Aunt Abbey slid a tray of kolaczki out of the oven. Stand-up fans whirred. It was cool in the kitchen, but my aunt was as red and sweaty as if she'd been sunning on the roof. She waved me over.

I asked her if the bathroom was occupied by the enemy.

She offered me an apricot kolaczky. "Around here, what isn't?"

We each ate one. They disintegrated, their sweetness subtle, then full, then lasting. The bottle of Chopin had vanished, which made me feel like I'd passed a basketball right between the legs of Uncle Lech to Aunt Abbey. I scratched my beard, hoping she'd comment on it, and asked about her birthday, how she was feeling.

"Forty-one," she said. "The forties. The decade of the unveiling of your limitations, of the polishing of them. Of trying to position your limitations into bridges that reach beyond themselves."

I asked her what she meant.

She said that after journeying through one full year in the forties she could clearly see the thirties sealed off behind her. In those thirties wound a number of named paths that she would not be taking with her life, named paths that ended in roles that she would not be playing. Although American optimism demanded that one meet this situation with denial, it was fact, and facts of this order were best understood when impaled on shining pins and stuck to one's chest. "When you turn thirty next spring," she said, "you'll feel what I mean, a little. Only less severely, less serenely. Help me find a spatula."

We searched the vases, parting their bouquets of colored pencils and wooden spoons.

My father had eleven years on my aunt. This gap gave their brother-sister conflicts a buried father-daughter fault line. To my brother she was Auntie Big Sister, friend and family, and to me she was that, too, but in a truth-telling-babysitter sort of way, the cool semi-stranger I wished would take my parents' place for more than one night at a time. As a teenager I found ways to ditch my mom and dad's separate family gatherings and I never saw her. I graduated. She heard, probably from my brother, that I wanted to move to the city—she knew a landlord with a cheap place in Edgewater nine blocks from her even cheaper place in Edgewater—so she met me there and I signed the lease. For the next six and a half years I trudged through undergrad, scraping up courses at community colleges and UIC, while my aunt made art and wrote grants, managed galleries and local co-ops, and dated a diverse ecosystem of men. Once a month she'd text me on a weekend—"I regret to inform you that you have canceled your plans for the day"— and take me to an opening or an experimental six-hour play or a bookstore poetry reading or a protest downtown, and afterwards we'd order mixed drinks at arty bars or PBR tallboys at not-so-divey dives, and she'd force me to try sushi or Nigerian fried goat or Bengali sweets or real-deal Chinatown Chinese, and if we talked about our personal lives, she'd knead the surface of our circumstances until they surrendered stimulating big-picture questions, deep feeling, deep thinking, as if all it took to find the work of art in anything was an act of careful framing. Whatever we did, wherever we went, she'd show me favorite sights, "unintended auto-masterworks": a stately tree trunk's slow absorption of the meshing of a fence; a lone bike wheel U-locked to a gate, rusting in streaks, sheaves of ivy twisting the rim into an urban wreath; a flattened rat, rug-like, its spinal cord and pelvis mysteriously intact, risen somehow to the top of the pelt; the drawing of a two-lane street chalked by kids onto the sidewalk, concrete signifying concrete, the city itself at the center of their play. I graduated. I worked a job I didn't like. When I told my aunt I was thinking of applying to grad school, she turned a walk through the Northwestern campus into a surprise meeting with the chair of the anthropology department. He seemed to think it was a date. Her hair shone, rayed with silver-gray by her early thirties, but her face, figure, and carriage were youthful, and this supposed contradiction pulled the crank on a wheel of charm that induced men and women between the ages of twenty-one and seventy into offering to buy her drinks.

I was there the night she said yes to a middle-aged artist named Lech.

He bought me a bourbon, too, to make me stay.

They talked performance art, politics, lactic fermentation crocks, and "the male impulse versus the female impulse" in American cinema. They debated which Polish traits were most invisible to Poles and which Polish-American traits were most invisible to Polish Americans. This first stage of their flirtation was almost entirely intellectual, as if they both preferred to pretend that they were bodiless. Every now and again, Lech looked me in the eye and solicited my opinion, but when I gave it, he didn't listen to my words, he listened to how I said them. I didn't like this, and I sensed my aunt's urge to be alone with him, so I slid the bartender money for the next round and stood up to go. The man who would become my uncle rose to protest or to fake-protest, but stopped before he spoke, paled, and sat back down. Then he fell to the floor. We called an ambulance.

My aunt looked in on him the next day—he'd suffered (or fake-suffered) a blood clot.

A week later he proposed.

28

Stanley Recalls the First Year of Aunt Abbey's Marriage to Uncle Lech

After a one-month engagement, they married. My dad and my mom and my brother and Busia and I didn't go—our invitations arrived a week before the wedding. The wedding was in Kraków.

"The man is a thief," said Busia.

My dad smiled. "What do we do, call the cops?"

"No," she said. "Sever his hands."

We were making pierogi at my dad's. My dad fed the dough through the press, Busia cut the pressed strips into circles, and my brother and I packed, shaped, and sealed the circles into pierogi. We made two kinds, like always: potato with browned butter, and pork with onions and mushrooms and cabbage. Outside, falling snow whirled across the yards of the subdivision. A father and a son one house over rolled up a family of snowmen.

"That's not enough, Ma," said my dad. "We'd have to pop out his eyeballs, too."

"And probably cut off his ears," I said.

"He doesn't get to keep his nose, does he?" said my brother.

My dad and my brother and I were laughing. Nobody had really wanted to go to the wedding.

"Man is a beast that laughs," said Busia.

My dad woofed.

Busia kept cutting circles and slapping them onto the table. "Work," she said.

My dad growled and snarled.

"Get the muzzle!" said my brother. "Get the leash!"

My dad grabbed my wrist and howled.

I grabbed his—I howled right back.

After the wedding, Aunt Abbey moved out of her Edgewater apartment, where she'd lived for over a decade, to my uncle's apartment-and-studio in Pilsen. Her spontaneous invites to art events slowed, then stopped. I emailed her about gallery openings in Edgewater and Rogers Park, thinking she might like to pop back to the old neighborhood, and I texted her about festivals in Pilsen and Bridgeport, thinking she might find the South Side more doable, but she responded too late or not at all. I didn't hold this against her. She was reshuffling.

Nearly a year later, she texted: did I want to do a bike tour of Pilsen murals? I rushed down. We rode around the neighborhood and saw a dozen stunning murals on apartment buildings and abandoned factories, on underpasses and auto repair shops. The guide, an achy old man, provided layers of historical and cultural context, including anecdotes about the artists, almost all of whom he personally knew.

Afterwards my aunt and I grabbed tacos from Carnitas Don Pedro and devoured them in the shady dugout of a baseball field, in a park near her place. Kids at the edge of the outfield jogged through soccer drills. An elotes lady rolled her clanging cart across Eighteenth.

My aunt was more trim and toned than I'd ever seen her, but had a staggered stare, like she'd been socked by a ghost. She wore a loose T-shirt and a pair of paint-speckled shorts, which meant that she'd come straight from painting, but she was loaded up with new jewelry, all of it amber, richly whorled necklaces and bracelets and rings. Every piece looked like an imploded galaxy. We discussed the most spectacular mural we saw, a garage-door work that depicted Aztecs imprisoned in a burning space station. The artist had been up-to-date on archaeology—one of the figures' faces, modeled on the knife-tongued god at the center of the iconic Aztec sun stone, had been painted a super-glossy black. Although the sun stone had long since lost its paint by the time it was discovered, a very recent study had made the case that the god's face had been black, or perhaps unpainted. He was dying, the archaeologists argued. He was being killed by an eclipse.

Our guide had positioned the mural as a critique of Chicago Public Schools. The artist, he noted with melancholy pride, was his niece.

"His niece has vision," said my aunt. "If I had just half her vision, I'd be twice the artist."

I wondered if our guide had ever wanted to be an artist. "The way he talked about his niece," I said.

"I've seen it many times before," said my aunt. "He's a person who at one point told himself that he wanted to 'Be an Artist.' What he was truly telling himself, though, was that he wanted to 'Be the *Idea* of an Artist.'"

"I don't see much of a difference," I said. "You need the idea. The idea takes you to the thing itself."

"But if you anchor yourself in the idea, you've anchored yourself in wanting. Not in the work. Once you're there, if you're not careful, the wanting will replace everything. You'll start to want to believe that the idea can replace *you*—that it can complete you. It doesn't matter what the idea is, the Idea of an Artist, the Idea of a Partner, the Idea of a Family. You'll steer yourself into a cloud. You might not notice right away, but when you do, on your own or with someone's help, it's over. You fall out of the sky."

I said I didn't follow.

"I left Lech," she said.

She shifted to sit cross-legged on the bench.

I was too surprised to know what to say.

She said that Lech was everything she'd wanted in a

partner-in-art-and-in-life, so much so that when she was with him, she was without space, without mystery. "Being without space, being without mystery—for an artist, that is not sustainable. Such conditions cripple the process."

To me this sounded like the cover page to a more painful truth. But what I said was that I was sorry to hear it. I asked her how she was holding up.

A plane surged overhead, gray and low, descending.

My aunt stared at the ballfield. She seemed to be weighing what it would do to our friendship if she were to tell me more.

I asked her where she was staying.

"I'm moving out at the end of the week," she said.

I gathered up the taco wrappers. When I stuffed them in the dugout trash can, I accidentally displaced more garbage—two handfuls clabbered out and into the dirt, mostly plastic cups and straws and snack bags. I gathered that up, too.

My aunt said, "Tell me about your girlfriend."

Ro and I had been together for a month or two. Everything was easy.

"Plenty of space and mystery so far," I said.

I didn't mean for it to come out sounding flippant, but it did.

"You don't believe me," she said, smiling without smiling. "You don't believe what I'm saying about art, about love, about me and Lech."

I said I didn't know much about them as a couple.

She asked me if I was ready to know.

I said that if she wanted to tell me, I'd listen.

She told me about Lech's first major project, a logistically complex piece he'd put together ten years ago when he lived in Poland. The title translated to *Nothing About Us, Without Us*, a phrase associated with a sixteenth-century legal ruling that granted democratic powers to Polish nobles. Over time, however, the phrase had attached itself to something else, the "nothing" and the "without us" coming to signify a particularly Polish frustration with the fact that at certain moments in history the nature of the nation's existence had been determined by foreign powers. Lech hired a young artist, and with his permission, the artist's friends, family members, and long-term girlfriend. The project's intended duration was one month. Lech began to implement "interpersonal partitions"—one by one, the people closest to the artist were phased out of his life, symbolically and concretely, collapsing his "metaphysical borders." They stopped returning his calls and meeting up with him. Lech covertly removed meaningful objects from the artist's apartment: framed photos, favorite shirts and mugs, old sketchbooks, gifts and notes from his girlfriend. Week by week, the methods increased in intensity; the important people who had pulled out of his life passed through it again, but on the edges, and without acknowledging him. The project ended three days early with the artist's death from an overdose.

"He had selected the young man, in part, because of his addiction to pain meds, which he'd developed after complications from a vasectomy," said my aunt. "Lech felt that these factors could not be more metaphorically apt."

After *Nothing About Us, Without Us*, Lech left Poland. Not because of the artist's death, or the artist's family's lawsuits, but because of the national art community's failure to respond, positively or negatively, to the piece's exhibition. Poland was not the place for performance art, he decided.

"Am I a human person who can love a human person like that?" said my aunt.

She twisted off one of her two amber rings. It was thick and sleek, the inside inscribed with words I couldn't read.

Then there was his near-death experience with the blood clot, she said, which, by his own account, had driven him to up the scale and the stakes of every subsequent project, which, she admitted, had led to upsetting moral questions.

"Am I a committed artist who can admire—and live with,

and work with—and see with, and know with—a committed artist like that?"

She plunked the ring into the trash can.

"I used to be sure I wanted to be. I used to be sure I *was*."

She popped off one of her two amber bracelets and one of her two amber necklaces.

"His English is perfect," she said. "The accent is a performance."

She balled up the bracelet with the necklace and dropped them into the trash can.

"I'm moving out at the end of the week," she said again.

Two weeks later I texted. No response.

A month later I called. Nothing.

Two months after that she sent out a group invite to a combination birthday/housewarming party at her and Uncle Lech's new house in Rogers Park. It was the first that any of us had heard about this move.

"I was mistaken," she said when I arrived.

None of her amber jewelry was in sight.

"You found mystery and space again," I said.

She smiled: a real smile.

"I gave it up," she said.

She seemed happy.

I hugged her.

29

Stanley Recounts Uncle Lech's Proposal at His Aunt Abbey's Birthday Party

"I attended T's show last night," said my aunt, opening two drawers at once, searching them for a spatula. "T is the single most committed young actor I've seen this year. Everything about her is rooted. She is a root. She roots into the soils below the soils, the richest, rarest earth."

I checked the cabinets under the sink: detergent, rubber gloves, mannequin heads. My aunt was right. I'd never thought about T in those terms, but onstage, it was her stability that stood out. Everything in her expressions, movements, and speech suggested dimensions of depth, even when she spontaneously rehearsed, practicing her lines and blocking in the bedroom or on walks through the neighborhood.

"Outside of the stage, as well," said my aunt. "A deep ease."

T had loved talking to my aunt. We'd all gone to lunch a few times, and the two of them had interacted like friends reuniting, not like strangers getting to know each other.

I continued to act like nothing was wrong with my life: I rummaged through a wicker basket piled with cookbooks and obscene finger puppets.

My aunt discovered a spatula in the pocket of a smock.

She flicked it about, as if it were wet.

This was the time to tell her that I had proposed to T, that T had said no and moved out, that T and I were on a break.

"After the show," she said, gesturing with the spatula, encouraging herself to talk, "T invited me around the corner with the cast. She let me buy her a drink at the bar. We shared a joint in the alley. We discussed a few things."

I stopped.

The look my aunt gave me wasn't sympathetic, but it said, Sympathetic.

Then it said, Apologetic.

T might have told her everything.

It hurt. I tried not to show it.

My aunt spatulaed kolaczky off the cookie sheet and onto a rack. A few flipped awry, to the floor. Neither of us made a move to pick them up.

Instead of saying, "What did T tell you," I said, "I'll be right back."

The bathroom was partly open. I knocked and nudged the door, finding the space unoccupied, just the sink and the toilet and the stand packed with foreign-language tour guides to the United States. On the wall was a hand-drawn shadow of a man in a hat and trench coat. He held a purse as if it were a briefcase. When I turned to close the door the doorway was full of Uncle Lech.

He snapped a picture with an old camera, the flash explosive.

I slammed and locked the door. The figure of my uncle stayed in my vision in searing negative. Pissing, I felt the echoes of my father's anger—I saw my father smashing the camera, smashing Uncle Lech, and smashing through the door on the way to his truck, to traffic, to the condo he'd built himself and hated.

I flushed the toilet. My father would never do the things that I imagined.

"Stasiu," said Uncle Lech as I opened the door.

Instead of the camera he held the bottle of Chopin and two shot glasses. His shirt and tie evoked the 1940s or '50s. He had a serious, pale, and pitted face, and a sloppy mustache that hid his mouth. He looked like a handsome actor who'd been made up ugly.

His eyes were blue lights on broken ice.

He said, "I offer proposal."

Every now and again he pitched "proposals" to my dad and brother, and because my dad refused to speak or listen to him, I'd get the scoop from my brother, who always listened, laughing, as Uncle Lech invited him to spend an afternoon wearing a tape recorder while riding the Red Line from Howard to Ninety-Fifth and back, or a day modeling for an inspirational rags-to-riches mural he planned to paint on a train car he'd found knocked over near defunct tracks on the West Side, or a night in an office chair on the roof of the Stock Exchange wearing suits and eating steaks. In the four years we'd known him this was the first he'd asked me. Whatever I'd felt about being photographed in the bathroom hardened inadvisably into pride.

We sat on stools at the breakfast bar. Aunt Abbey powder-sugared kolaczki at the counter, not looking at us.

Uncle Lech filled the glasses. They were doubles. He chewed on his mustache hairs, clicking them with his teeth. "You suffer unemployment?"

I'd been unable to score a full-time job since dropping out of grad school and everybody knew it.

"You have not yet traveled out of country?"

I hadn't.

"You desire to travel out of country, to gain employment?"

I asked him where.

"Prague."

I must've gone as red as my aunt.

He raised his glass. "It will not be that you will be in over your head," he said. He drank. I didn't. He licked vodka droplets from his mustache, observing me. I wanted him to know that I knew what he was up to, that if I agreed, it'd be because

I'd position my own interests before his, at the cost of his. I did my best to press this into how I stared back.

He belched.

Aunt Abbey set a plate of kolaczki between us: cherry, almond, poppy seed, prune.

"Dziękuję," he said tenderly, touching her waist.

I couldn't remember another time I'd seen him thank her.

"Thanks," I said, wanting her to look at me.

She looked at no one and said nothing and left the kitchen for the backyard. The screen door whapped. My brother hollered something silly. My body clenched: I wanted badly to be outside. Not so much to know what joke had just been made, but to be taken away from myself by it.

Uncle Lech put his hand on my shoulder like my brother had. His fingers were hot. He explained that he'd invested in a Prague apartment near Old Town Square, an expensive venture. He needed someone to apartment-sit and to facilitate the move-in of a tenant. He'd come to trust me.

"You are actual," he said.

He would pay for my round-trip ticket. For three days I would stay in his apartment, my duties minimal, and on the last day the tenant would move in and I would move out. I could stay abroad as long as I liked—to visit other cities, other countries—and my return flight could be arranged from anywhere. He'd need me there at the end of August. He'd pay five thousand dollars.

I drank my vodka. "T is going to be in Prague then. But you knew that."

"When I was young man," he said, "I did not know why I did action. I pretend I did. Make money, make art, make love. Crack a man. Immigrate. Pick up broken garbage and put them where you live. Lie. All because of hiding and pretending! The man in the basement behind the noise door that is locked and eating the one key himself while shouting, No, this is not what I am doing. Now I am not young man: the reason why I do action is that I do not know. I do not know! I love Abbey—I do not know how—I do not say that I know, saying some thing that is made up—I very basically love her. I kiss her on the mouth. We touch. It is observed. This is my development, this is not your development: you understand. You are actual, Stasiu. Today you know why you do action. You go to graduate school, it is not good to you, you leave. Your mother talks, it is not good to you, you leave. What is it that you cannot leave, when you, the actual man, are knowing?"

This was an inventive misinterpretation of my personality.

I asked him what Aunt Abbey thought about the proposal.

"Hand wash hand," he said. "Leg support leg."

I gripped his arm, like he'd gripped my shoulder, only harder, and in doing so I elbowed the plate of kolaczki off the table. It broke on the floor with a bang.

I said, "I know what you're doing. You're fucking with me. That's fine, that's expected. But T has to have nothing to do with this. If you involve her in any way, I'll lose my shit. Me losing my shit will be bad for you, and your artists, and whatever your fucking project is, and me."

His face transformed, stage by stage: disarming warmth, distant wisdom, paternal fondness. It was like watching a mask get made.

I asked him if he understood me.

"I do," he said, but the way it came out, he might as well have said, "I love you."

His intensity was unnerving.

I leaned over to pick up the shattered pieces of the plate, but he stopped me.

"I will fix it," he said.

30

Stanley Recalls the Flight to Prague

The plane hummed. My head felt vacuum-packed. I tugged open a bag of peanuts and they all jumped into my lap. The teenager in the middle seat, who hadn't once looked at me, looked at me and scowled. She was wearing pajamas and eye shadow.

My brother had said that there were seriously awful things we didn't know about Uncle Lech and that it was probably pretty dumb for me to go to Prague. "I know you know that," he said. The L whoosh-rattled in the background. He was downtown, strolling back to the office from his lunch break at the Pittsfield Café, a diner he'd invited me to meet him at on more than one occasion. I sensed, not for the first time, that our dad, who had given us the impression that he knew disturbing secrets about Uncle Lech—disturbing secrets he kept from us, a protective parental act for which he expected (but never outright requested) respect—had shared some of what he knew with my brother. My brother must have promised not to say anything to me. Because he always kept his promises, I didn't hassle him. His discomfort was evident. I also sensed that although he thought it was pretty dumb (and possibly dangerous) for me to go to Prague, he wanted to believe that it'd be nourishing for me, just like he wanted to believe that it was nourishing (though dangerous) for me to get into fistfights in high school. "Just think about it this way," he said, persuading himself, "because you know the kind of shitshow you're walking into, you should be able to ignore it okay, to step away from all the crazy scheming and shake out a few good times." He reminded me that a few years ago he'd toured Prague with Guillerma, his ex-girlfriend. He said, "You'll dig the dark history."

"Would you go," I said.

"You should ask Mom. She goes to Prague like every other year! Hey—when you're there, she'll be in Kraków, not too far away."

I didn't say anything.

"Our circumstances are different!" said my brother.

"If they were the same."

"The violin does not play for everyone," he croaked, imitating Busia.

He laughed, I didn't.

"I don't know," he said. "Probably. Yes."

My father had said that I was stupid, more stupid than he'd imagined, and here in one decision was all the proof he'd ever needed.

I asked him why my decision was so stupid.

He said that the question itself was stupid.

I said, "What happened to your neck."

"Work."

"You must be stupid enough to think that I believe that."

He stayed silent to make me listen closely. Then he hung up.

I called him back and left a voice mail in which I said that his habit of not telling me or my brother important information about himself and Mom and Aunt Abbey and Uncle Lech was stupid, more stupid than he could imagine, and although to him it might seem manly, it was in fact cowardly. It was a go-fuck-yourself. Go fuck yourself.

This wasn't the first time I'd said something like this to my father, but it was the first time I felt I might puke afterwards.

I thought of how Aunt Abbey had been evasive and embarrassed, of how she'd looked at me in her kitchen and hadn't looked at me later. I started to feel pre-betrayed by her, a feeling that sawed at my insides. I didn't want to call her but I did.

"There is nothing like international travel to remind you that you are thoroughly American," she said.

None of the embarrassment that had clung to her at her party was sticking to her voice. It was as if we'd bounced back to where we'd always been.

When she was my age, she explained, she'd gone to Gdańsk for an arts festival. A locally famous painter invited her to dinner. They discussed American and European history, and through that, American and European politics, and the only thing that they agreed on was the fact that almost all of their underlying principles, individually speaking, were opposed. At the end of the night he asked her where she'd learned to speak the Polish that she knew. She said she was Polish-American. He shook his head: "You are American-American."

"That man told the truth," said my aunt.

Someone near her tuned a trumpet.

I said, "T told you that I proposed to her. She told you that she said no and moved out."

The trumpet oomped and blarted.

"Because you know what happened," I said, "you persuaded Uncle Lech to propose that I go to Prague at the same time that T will be there for her show. You were thinking that this could help me and T's relationship, but now you're having second thoughts. You're worried that the project is going to get too dangerous. You feel bad about what's going to happen to me or to T when we're there, but not bad enough to tell me what to expect. Or that I shouldn't go."

"That's almost right," she said.

I was shaking.

"If I shouldn't go, you need to tell me, right now."

She asked if I remembered the time at a Logan Square gallery when we saw a blindfolded performance artist place her hand on the white wall by the entrance to an empty exhibition space, press hard, and trace the perimeter by dragging her fingertips slowly, the invisible line gradually darkening into visibility with her blood. Did I remember how no one in the audience followed her the whole time, including us—at her pace, it would've taken her two or three hours to get back to where she started—and therefore, how the only witness to the entirety of the piece, thanks to the blindfold, was the piece itself?

"Your aunt is for the art, for the art above it all," she said. "If I lose that I lose my means of re-seeing myself."

In her voice was a plea.

I stayed silent to make her listen closely. I said, "It's good that it's too late for you to have children."

She didn't speak. I hung up.

This was the first time I'd said something like this to my aunt. I rushed to the sink and gripped the rim, prepared to puke. Nothing came up.

I wrote an email to T about the trip. She wrote back that I was nuts to agree to three days in my uncle's apartment, a closed set that he could so completely manipulate—did I really think that anything good would come of this?—but yes, of course, why not, between shows she'd look forward to a cup of coffee or a drink. I selected my flights. Work picked up, an apartment-complex renovation in the South Loop. Every morning, Niko pointed at what he wanted me to rip out. He'd say, "Have at it." On the L to and from the site, clacking through neighborhoods I'd never been to, I thought of T in Prague. "Prague" was independent of "Chicago," of the Chicago places where T had been and now wasn't, of the Chicago places where T now was. "Prague" was a place that was a word, a word that I would try to make mean "a do-over." It had a history and a culture that I didn't intend to understand. I didn't pretend to want to know what "Prague" was like, but I pretended to know how T and I would be when we were there: we would be the very best versions of ourselves. I busted up a countertop and I tore out a sink. I dragged an oven down a driveway. "You're a monster!" said Niko. T texted me. there was something she needed to talk about, it was complex, could I meet in person? I ducked out of earshot of Niko and called. On the L I called again. At home I texted. The next day she emailed to set up a drink at the Hopleaf. The night of the drink, she canceled. She apologized and rescheduled. She canceled the reschedule. Then she emailed to say that she was sorry to ask, but would it be okay if Manny crashed with me at my uncle's place in Prague? It wasn't unusual for T to suggest logistical rearrangements, but it was unusual for her to suggest them on someone else's behalf, especially when she herself was not involved in the rearrangement. I texted, "Call me now please." I waited a day, and called; I waited three days, and called again; I waited a week and called and left an angry voice mail in which I said that I knew she'd told my aunt about the marriage proposal and the move-out, I wish she hadn't, but she could do what she wanted to do including deciding to participate in my uncle's project without telling me about it. "I want to be wrong about this," I said in the message. "Tell me I'm wrong." I gouged a wall by walking past it with a crowbar on Monday, and I whacked my thumb with a hammer on Tuesday, and I rear-ended an old lady's station wagon in the parking lot of the Jewel on Wednesday, and I stayed home "sick" from work and sat on the floor in front of the TV thinking about what things meant and how they mattered and where they matched up with what I wanted versus what I thought I wanted on Thursday. On Friday I texted T and said, "Manny can stay with me." She texted back that I'd guessed right—she'd talked to my aunt after a show and had said some things to her she maybe shouldn't have, she'd been drunk and high and sad, not that those were excuses, and then a week later my uncle approached her as she was walking out of her apartment late one night, he was wearing a wet trench coat even though it wasn't raining, and he invited her to play a role in his Prague project, which he said would be his most meaningful work to date, which involved me. She of course refused, she said. Then my uncle offered to pay to keep her from telling me that he'd contacted her at all. It was a lot of money. But everything about it struck T as icky, and she was sorry to say that even the encounter with my aunt, in hindsight, felt conspiratorial. So she told him no. Manny's visit to Prague, though, was outside of this. She would've been happy to put him up herself, but she was staying with her cast and crew in a dinky rented apartment in which there'd be no room for even one more person. Manny was arriving on the same day I was and only planned to stay a night or two. But she understood my reaction, she said, who was she to ask for a favor when we hadn't even met for lunch like we said we would, it'd been how long since the move-out? Which reminded her, had I found a roommate to help with the rent yet, her offer to pay half for another month still stood. I said that if Manny staying with me in my uncle's apartment in Prague meant that I would see her, then Manny could stay with me. She said you're sure? I said see you there, break a leg. She said sorry for the imposition. But thank you. And be careful.

I received texts from my uncle (pictures of dummies in dark suits and dresses), and texts from an unknown number (pictures of tables piled with film equipment and desktop computers), and texts from a second unknown number (pictures of spreadsheets and call sheets), and voice mails from a third unknown number (I didn't listen to them).

More texts and voice mails from more unknown numbers followed, a new one every other day, and then a new one every day, and then a new one several times a day.

I deleted the pictures and messages, I blocked the numbers.

A week before the flight, I texted Torrentelli and Barton. It'd been some time since we'd all met up at Huettenbar. I arrived early and claimed a table up front, under broad windows opened to the street. Men and women passed by on Lincoln, tugging dogs and shoving strollers. This was the time to tell my two friends that I was the owner of an unwanted engagement ring, that I'd been living alone for almost a month, that I was trying to believe that a "break" was different from a "breakup," and that I'd allowed my aunt and uncle and possibly T to manipulate me into traveling to a foreign country to supply material for a performance art project that would almost certainly produce nothing but a complicated spectacle of confusion, humiliation, and rage. I ordered an easy golden beer. Torrentelli and Barton came through the door together, laughing. They both worked in the Loop. We caught up—Torrentelli, a paralegal, had switched firms for marginally better pay and a much better boss; Barton, a manager, had been promoted to what he'd hoped would be a more stimulating position within his company but was turning out to be even more mission-less and soul-damning; that morning I'd sledgehammered a wall between two bedrooms. "Does the beard make your dick bigger?" said Barton. "Let's ask T," said Torrentelli, texting. I turned to the window. "Aren't actors supposed to date people with full-time jobs?" said Barton. "Or at least people who look good in beards?" Torrentelli ordered Jägerbombs. "Look, we're in college!" said Barton. "Stan is," said Torrentelli, proud. Barton cupped his hands over his mouth and said to our bartender, "Stan studies dead people because Stan is a dead person, metaphorically." Torrentelli's phone babbled. She rolled her eyes. "It's Mickey," she said. "You guys don't know Mickey." "Nope," said Barton. Torrentelli answered with "What happened?" and stepped outside. She loitered at our window. By her occasional glances, she signaled to us that this unknown friend of hers was not only boring, but also self-absorbed and annoying. The guilt that I felt at that moment was so sharp and hard that I stood up to leave. Barton, thinking I was going for another beer, bought me one. He gave me a worried frown. "You just keep taking it," he said. "What the fuck is up?"

I said that what the fuck was up was a stick up my ass named Barton. I tried to be funny about it.

"Something's wrong with Stan," said Barton to Torrentelli, when she came back. "He's trying to be funny."

Torrentelli took ahold of my hands like she was the pope.

"Come clean before the Lord God Jesus Pilsner," she said.

Barton made the sign of the cross with a pint.

If I told them right then, I knew, I wouldn't go.

I bowed my head in mock supplication. "I confess: I have no friends."

"Only us two fuckfaces," said Barton.

"Amen," said Torrentelli.

The night before the flight my father called me twice. He left two voice mails that I didn't listen to. While I packed my bag on the bed, I saw that I was shaking again. I said to myself: You are afraid to hear concern in his voice. You are afraid that what he says and how he says it will make you stay in this apartment in which you now live by yourself. You don't want to stay in this apartment. You want to be a man who can move out.

Everything you are thinking you are thinking yourself into believing, I thought.

I winced at the smell of the sheets I hadn't washed since T had moved out.

I washed the sheets.

I banked my uncle's check.

I printed the ticket to T's show.

I didn't return the ring but I didn't pack it.

I didn't pack my phone.

I packed *Sacred Centers: New Perspectives on North American Burial Mounds*.

On the flight, I picked peanuts off my lap and ate them.

The teenager next to me adjusted her pillow in such a way that it brushed the side of my face on purpose. When I looked at her she pointed to the floor, to the dropped peanuts I'd ignored.

"I'm allergic," she said, sheepish.

I unbuckled and bent to pluck them up. An urge to weep kicked around on my face.

"Sorry," we said at the same time.

31

Stanley Accompanies Manny to a Restaurant

Manny had been listening to my description of my uncle's offer with interest, but acting otherwise. He'd traded my guide-book for *Sacred Centers*, and was thumbing through it, dwelling over diagrams.

There'd been no new phase in my uncle's project.

Manny had continued to interrupt me, to redirect my responses. Although I'd only covered what he could've already known from T, I didn't mention the marriage proposal or T's move-out.

"That's it," I said.

He closed my book dismissively.

"And yet," he said. "Why Prague?"

I opened another pop.

"Is it that your uncle, or your uncle's species of art, is met in Prague with an appreciation not to be found in Chicago, a city home to unsophisticated hordes of hot-dog-chomping everymen?"

He elaborated, including an aside about "faux-tender tough-guy sentimentality."

"Whereas Prague," he said, "with its cultural maturity, with its history of occupation, can claim a long-standing appetite for subversives and satirists. For art that mocks and undermines. Consider the legends of Zito. Consider the puppet theater. Consider Kafka, Hašek, Čapek. Consider Jára Cimrman."

He explained a recent national protest. I wasn't able to understand what was being protested, or how and why Manny talked the way he did, or Manny. I didn't want to, and I wasn't supposed to—every word he spoke was a point scored in a game he was playing with himself.

His phone, in his pocket, trilled with a text.

"In what state did you discover this apartment?" he said.

I told him that the one change I'd made was to load the fridge with pop and beer. I didn't tell him that Uncle Lech or a henchman artist had entered in my absence and switched the background on my laptop, that the place had had a pesticidal stink (now gone), or that the bedsheets were itchy to the touch.

I said, "By the way, the bed's yours."

Manny, picking at a crusty stain on the wall, paused to assess me. It was a deeply impersonal look, one I'd never seen him give to T. It made me want to pound him on the head with my can of pop.

I imagined pounding him on the head with my can of pop.

He said, "You are older than you used to be."

"You aren't."

"Ne," he agreed. "Restaurace, prosím!"

He picked a restaurant he'd seen on the way in, off-Square, but not by enough to be as inexpensive as it should have been. It was best, he argued, to begin one's culinary explorations in establishments that would safely confirm one's expectations. With such expectations secure, one could better risk the discovery of that most prized ephemerality, authenticity. We walked through Old Town Square. Manny described an inauthentic lunch in Florence that had enabled him to more completely appreciate an authentic dinner in Siena. Tourists strolled and lounged and posed for pictures, sitting at cafés or on cobblestones, content, weary, dreamy, bored, drunk, high. Some gathered aimlessly at an enormous monument out of which loomed ghostly oxidized copper figures. Others gathered expectantly at what looked like a medieval clock tower. "The Jan Hus Memorial," said Manny, interrupting himself as we passed these landmarks, "the Astronomical Clock. Sacrifice and time." The Square's borders were beautiful town halls and churches, a cross-century display of architectural styles. I didn't expect to feel anything in the Square, but I did, in spite of Manny: a sad grandeur that shamed me. In my life no such public space drew me to the center of my time. We left on side streets. The more they wended, the more they loosened, losing foot traffic. We found the restaurant and took lopsided stone steps down into it, way down, the dining room a dark cellar dressed up as a lodge. It smelled like the inside of a sausage. Stags' heads and torches adorned the walls. Long tables buzzed with non-Czechs not speaking Czech. We were seated. Waiters in green aprons brought us water, pretzels, menus.

With the air of already knowing my answers, Manny solicited my opinion on the culture, cuisine, and character of the Czech people.

"What are your impressions, I wonder?"

I didn't tell him that I'd wandered into ordinary everyday Prague or that I'd day-tripped to a magnificent ossuary in Kutná Hora. What I told him was that I hadn't even been in the city for a day.

"Yes—what have you learned so far?"

32

Stanley Watches Manny Answer His Own Question

"The history of Prague is the history of three peoples, the Czechs, the Germans, and the Jews," said Manny.

"The most economically influential people—my people—were the Germans," said Manny.

"Today, Prague is controlled by American bankers," said Manny.

"Some say that Prague is controlled by the Russian *nouveau riche*, but that impression has been propagated by American bankers," said Manny.

"Since the Velvet Revolution, Prague has redirected its economy to tourism. Sixty-one percent of the city's economic transactions are touristic."

"Golden Praha!" said Manny.

"'Praha' refers to the Czech word for 'threshold,'" said Manny.

"Like all Slavic tongues, Czech appears coarse on the page," said Manny, presenting the menu, touching words, "hrášek—peas—květák—cauliflower. Pairs of consonants offensive to an English speaker. But in the mouths of the Czechs, the language sparkles. It is ice water."

The unsmiling waiter returned with a notepad. I ordered, interrupting Manny.

Manny placed the exact same order: one half-liter of

Krušovice Cerne, which the menu said was "The Royal Brewing Blackbeer," and a plate of vepřo-knedlo-zalo, "the National dish proud of Pork and Dump Lings." We shared looks of surprise. I'd never seen him eat and drink anything other than veggie wraps and Manhattans, and he'd never seen anyone come to the birthplace of the pilsner and not order it immediately.

"The Czechs consume more pivo per capita than any other people," said Manny. "You must drink the pilsner."

The Krušovice came, dark and heady, full and rich. It tasted nutritious.

Manny raised his glass and toasted to T, to the work ethic that had placed her on the important proving ground that was this festival. She was on the verge of a moment that might turn out to be a switching station to a superior track. Here she would meet new enablers. They might do for her what no one she'd known before could.

I said, "Na zdrowie."

"That's Polish."

I said no shit it was.

"Na zdraví," said Manny, frowning.

He drank most of his beer in one swig, set his hands on his hips, and burped. The smell of what he'd had for lunch twisted in my face. New enablers were half of "talent," he said. He was excited to press T for details on the young director-playwright she'd connected with, a rising star in the international theater community who'd been lauded for his experimental approach to addressing social issues.

"In his most recent play, he invites the audience to indict the actors. He appoints the audience to a position inside his narrative system of consequences." Manny glanced at his watch. "T is there now."

He said the playwright's name and the name of the play. Last I'd talked to T, we'd planned to have a drink after her show, which was tomorrow night, and although I was hoping to touch base with her earlier than that, I didn't expect to see her until then. Now it seemed important to see her sooner.

I suggested that we meet up with her after she was finished with tonight's play.

Manny put on a cold smile. "She has already committed to a late dinner with the director-playwright."

At the table next to us, a nicely dressed mass of English bros triple-fisted beer, whiskey, and champagne. It was a bachelor party. The bachelor, a handsome big-chinned man in a cracked plastic top hat, was loudly detailing the geography of his fiancée's vagina.

"I learned that you have decided not to return to graduate school," said Manny.

"I dropped out."

"And your current search for employment?"

"I do construction part-time, mostly demo."

"Demolition."

"'Demo' is short for 'demolition.'"

"Your field was anthropology."

"Archaeological anthropology."

"The social sciences," he declared. "To seek the truth that is objective, until that truth objectively changes, one study at a time."

I said that ancient cultures had reasons for doing the things they did. Many of these reasons were unknown to us. But the more evidence that we discovered, the more conclusions we could draw from studying that evidence; the more conclusions we collected, the closer we could come to the ancient cultures' reasons behind even their most mysterious practices.

Manny said, "The social sciences: the process of the simplification of human society."

"Truth is a process of simplification," I said, quoting Dr. Madera.

Manny laughed.

33

Stanley Remembers Another Instance of Manny's Laugh

We'd sat down to unlace our bowling shoes. I'd won both games we'd played. The fluorescent lights came on, bleaching the bowling alley into looking like a high school basement.

Manny was laughing at a story T was telling.

T pantomimed a scared person peeking into a box.

Manny laughed much harder, his laughter ascending itself as if it were its own staircase. This was T's favorite "Manny-ism": watching it, she snorted. A smile began to pry at my face and I fought it like you fight a sneeze. Manny removed his glasses, wiped at tears.

I asked Manny's friend Inna how she was liking America. "I do not," she said. "But I do not like many places."

She popped a cigarette in her mouth and went outside to smoke it. I followed her. I'd quit a week ago but asked for one.

"This is all I have," she said, showing me her empty pack.

It was cold. A bus across the street sucked its doors shut and took off, its passengers well-lit, bobbing.

Inna offered me a drag and I accepted, breathing deep. She motioned for me to hang on to it for a while. I remembered that she was a student and asked her what she studied.

"International finance systems," she said. "But I do not think that I will finish my dissertation."

"What's stopping you."

"Myself."

She smiled. I gave her back her cigarette.

"I have a question about T's appearance," she said.

Everyone in my family and all of my friends had at some point asked about T's ethnic background, most of them prefacing the question with a wrong guess, which T found annoying, which I increasingly found annoying, so I was grateful for Inna's don't-presume-anything approach. I said that one of T's parents was black and Puerto Rican and one was Chinese and white mutt.

Inna said no, she wanted to know was it challenging to love a beautiful woman.

I felt ashamed. I apologized. "Yes," I said, though I'd meant to say no.

"As challenging as it is to love a woman who is not?"

Inna had a pretty face with troubled skin, and her way of carrying herself, though not unattractive, wasn't attractive to me. But when she said this, my blood jumped. Her eyes had deepened with a meaning I wasn't sure I caught.

I said that whoever you happened to love was hard to love.

To say that a challenging activity was challenging was to not say anything, she said. She began to tell a story about an American poet she used to know, a man who'd staggered in and out of love with her, who'd once spent nine straight hours riding the ring that was the St. Petersburg subway, alone, writing what he said were "secret missile love poems."

I asked a question, I forgot what, then T and Manny emerged, exuberant, reminiscing:

The time they dumped a can of night crawlers into the bully Kevin Rovik's backpack!

The time they Photoshopped the bully Kevin Rovik's yearbook picture onto an image of the sweaty body of Richard Simmons, whom he resembled, and left copies all over school!

The time they planted a peanut-butter-and-dogshit sandwich in the bully Kevin Rovik's lunch bag, disguised as his daily

PBJ—wrapped in the same wax paper and on the same wheat bread and halved on the same diagonal—and he bit into it!

They always carried off every scheme and never were suspected once and wouldn't ever regret what they did to the bully Kevin Rovik, that ogre, that lumbering dumbfuck, that proud-of-his-own-stubborn-ignorance shitsack, who had it coming!

T slugged Manny in the arm, harder than she'd slug me, but for the same reason. He laughed his laugh to the next floor, and then to the roof.

34

Stanley Eats a Meal and Takes a Lengthy Constitutional with Manny

His laughter went up a story but was nowhere near the roof.

Our food came: gravy-rich slabs of roast pork, spongy dumplings, and a heap of hot sauerkraut. We picked up our forks and knives. Manny chewed with his eyes closed and his mouth open, visibly restraining himself from moaning with pleasure in a way that was worse than if he'd actually been moaning with pleasure.

We finished our beers at the same time, halfway through our plates, and when the waiter appeared at that very instant, Manny ordered two pilsners, prosím. I stopped the waiter and told him in English that I wanted another Krušovice. He scratched it on his notepad.

Manny explained his position on the relationship between truth and complexity. His argument, which he'd been developing as a "subtle secondary thesis" in his dissertation, was that the standard for objective-seeming subjective truths was the extent to which they discretely honored complexity. Did you need a truth to feel true? Then that truth must address complexity, but indirectly, in the dark, under the table. He licked gravy from between the tines of his fork. I asked why overtness had to be avoided, why directness didn't lead effectively to truth. Pleased, he referenced theorist after theorist, only one I'd heard of, as if his goal wasn't so much to prove his point as it was to prove how thoroughly he knew the names of the people related to his point. Manny attended a historically prestigious university in Berlin, and although I used to know what he studied, all I could remember at the moment was T saying that he wanted to be a terrible diplomat, like his mother.

"You want to be a terrible diplomat," I said.

"Diplomats are robots in crisis. They are required by their government to go against their programming, to do the things that authentic human beings do not prefer to do. I will do business."

"Business is authentic."

"Only money is authentic. Money, and actors."

He argued that authenticity was representation: coins, bills, and credit cards weren't wealth itself, they represented it, and in this representation achieved an identity more concrete than the identity of the abstract power they represented. The representation actually *was* the power it represented, whereas the power it represented was literally immaterial. So too with actors: most people, to most people, were fictional. Actors made strangers more real than real strangers.

"Take these fellows," he said, indicating the bachelor party, as one of them stood and led the others in an incomprehensible fight song. The bachelor himself and one of his buddies, not fans of the team the song honored, but entertained by the performance, feigned looks of disgust. They pointed at each other across the table and pretended to puke.

Manny extrapolated, using these men to annotate his argument.

I interrupted him to say that he had a point, but that the way he stated it, in absolutes, made him sound more full of shit than he was. If he was using that strategy in his dissertation he was fucked.

He said that to be authentic was to be assolutamente pieno della merda.

I said that he was the real thing, then.

He pointed at me across the table and pretended to puke.

The waiter returned with three beers: the two that Manny had ordered and the one that I had. Manny talked about Italy, Italians, and the Italian language. "Italiano is so precise," he said. "La mia birra. Le miei birre."

He drank his second beer and then he drank the extra.

When the bill came he reviewed it, stopping his finger at every item. He handed it to me and said that this establishment didn't accept the two credit cards he carried, how unusual. I took out my wallet. He didn't offer to pay his part in cash, he didn't ask if I could cover him, he didn't say he'd pay me back. What he did was wait for me to pay.

Outside I smelled the roasted-meat stink of the restaurant on myself immediately. The sun hadn't set. Wide shadows pushed bright banks down the block. Manny stretched, touching his toes, and said that if he didn't take an after-dinner constitutional, his modeling career would be compromised. Somehow he was drunk. I bought a big bottle of Krušovice from a man working a food stand. A nearby pair of backpackers, sitting on a curb beside their packs, ripped into fried cheese sandwiches.

I imagined my brother and his ex, Guillerma, eating their own fried cheese sandwiches on their own patch of Prague curb a few years ago. I remembered the easy cut of their breakup.

"It was like there was a time limit," my brother had said when it happened, amazed. "We played hard for all four quarters. Then the whistle blew. We shook hands and went home on different buses."

I had liked Guillerma and I felt sad, sadder than my brother did.

"Don't worry," he'd said, noticing, laughing. "You'll get over it."

I followed Manny up a long road. Tourists slopped in and out of restaurants. City workers stepped down from networks of scaffolding attached to façades. Manny's eyes bugged with boyish joy. What was practiced here was not the restoration of history, he said, but history's *maintenance*. Did I consider what this difference implied about this culture? What prudence! What usefully employed pride! We came to a big pedestrian bridge. It cleared the river from out of some other century, carrying with it what looked like three dozen religious statues, set up on plinths and parceled out like the stations of the cross. Stout watchtowers with archways straddled both bridge-ends. People squeezed across its avenue in dense streams, dulled by or in awe of the scene they made, staring and pointing and arguing, laughing, pausing to take pictures of their faces in front of what they were seeing for the first time. I'd read about this bridge but couldn't remember its name. The dark river, the name of which I did remember, the Vltava, gave up no odor, no sour water sewer-waft. Manny evaluated each musician, artist, jeweler, and panhandler we passed. They advertised aggressively, their pleas personalized. We left the bridge and followed a street that shot uphill, climbing high into a corridor of closing gift shops, the customers puttering. A puppet show played out on a booth-like one-man stage. Manny announced the Castle, closed, and the St. Vitus Cathedral, closed. We came to a courtyard with a low wall. From there we saw the city as it appeared on the internet, its red roofs storing golden sheets of setting sunlight. Before us blazed a full-color catalogue in which one could find architectural exemplars of every style that was of consequence, said Manny. Did you care to admire the sturdy willpower of the Romanesque? The Gothic's vertical might? The voluted gables and sgraffito figures of the Renaissance? There stood the Baroque, the Rococo, the Imperial, the Classicist, the overrated-by-Americans Art Nouveau! Were you satisfied? You were satisfied? The sun set.

I'd never seen Manny this way.

"This little mother has claws!" he shouted, in his quoting-from-something voice. "Mystical, big, silent! Praha, nazdar! Ganz Praha ist ein Goldnetz von Gedichten!"

I swung my arms to stretch them, one at a time, and made sure to remember the route to this view. I would take T here. She would shudder with loving it. She would pin me with a hug.

"T might want to come here every night," I said.

Manny barely stopped himself from blurting out a response to this.

On our walk back down he maintained a busy silence. I felt him working out a monologue, preparing phrases. He tripped twice on cobblestones. At the bottom of the hill I shot my empty bottle like a free throw—it banged clean into the garbage can, no rim. I don't know how. I had hoped to miss.

Manny stopped in front of an alley.

"A confession," he said. "I am very skilled at 'reading' people. It is only rarely that I find that I have misjudged a social dynamic. My colleagues appreciate this—I am counsel to many men and women older than myself—however, when I met you, I could not determine what brought you to T and T to you, to say nothing of what keeps the both of you together. What interpersonal mechanic is in place? By what socio-romantic exchange system do you operate? I did not know. But now, tonight, after several hours with you, the truth is made obvious: you are that cliché of clichés, attractant-opposites! Initially I didn't trust this insight—to 'read' such a stereotypical arrangement seemed, to me, to indicate the malfunction of my judgment, or worse, the onset of intellectual laziness—but no, neither, all is confirmed: as your romantic opposite, T provides you, Stanley, with an *interesting instability*. Which you lack. Because you are boring. And you, as her romantic opposite, provide her with an *uninteresting stability*. Which she lacks, largely, but is made to think by various social forces that she requires. How can I dramatize it? You give her grocery store flowers. You give her a sunset over the city and a walk back the way you came. But T—T gives you a mad dash into the alley!"

He mad-dashed into the alley.

"Witches' fingers!" he said, waving his arms. "Bent and grown-broken! Mágico più nero della notte!"

Several feelings fell on top of me at once.

The first, the heaviest, was hope. From what Manny had said about me and T, and how he had said it, with disdainful admiration, I guessed that T hadn't told him about my rejected marriage proposal and her move-out and our break. If she hadn't mentioned these things to her old best friend, it might be because she was open to restarting our relationship.

The second feeling, which I felt at the same time as the first, was a stupefying out-of-body fear that the relationship I'd thought of as mysterious, challenging, and rewarding was in fact as simple as "opposites attract," "she's a catch," "you're a dud."

The third was that the first two feelings showed how much I needed to grow up.

The fourth was jet-lag drunk.

The fifth was me beginning to swerve away from myself.

The sixth, more thought than felt, was that the version of me and T that Manny imagined, "attractant-opposites," wasn't correct but was close, much closer than versions of us imagined by my brother, who called us "one hundred percent complementary," or by Torrentelli and Barton, who saw us as "somehow compatible," or by T's friends, who could only comment on how "super-supportive" we were of each other, or by my dad, who said, "Good for you," or by my mom, who implied that I should under no circumstances whatsoever break up with T, ever, even in the probable event of her cheating on me with a lawyer or a doctor, or by Aunt Abbey, who declared us "same-sighted."

Uncle Lech had only said: "Love is eating in the dark."

T would tell me to stop right there. She'd say: You're suggesting that what other people imagine is where we should be looking to figure out who we are.

No, I'd say. But we can learn from what other people *think* they see.

Stubborn Stanley, Angsty Wangsty Stanley: *we're* the experts on us! We know what no one who isn't us knows. Think about the things you've done that your friends and your family and me don't, can't, and won't imagine that you'd ever do, the things that we'd out of love or shock bet against you ever doing, the things that prove to you, if you take the time to think about them, that to a certain eerie degree everyone we know thinks we're someone we're not.

Yes. But what we mean when we say "I know you" accounts for those unknowns. That's the best we can do. That's knowing.

You're saying that now, but that's not what you believe outside this argument. That's not what you believe in real life!

Everything is real life!

Follow Manny!

I followed Manny into the alley. The buildings the alley cut between shot up, slivering the sky. No graffiti, no garbage. I didn't sprint to catch Manny but I hustled enough to keep him in sight.

A trio of hip young men passed him and then me, saying, "Marijuana, hash hash hash, marijuana."

"Ha!" said Manny.

I called his name.

We came to a nightclub with a short loud line. A man with a scabby head barked in an I've-got-your-back voice that he'd not only get us in, he'd get "hotties to sit with their butts in our laps." We crossed a narrow street dense with cars, a mini traffic jam, stereos pumping Top 40 and trance and Europop, one limo vibrating with cranked-up classical. Sketchy men beckoned us from passenger seats. Manny took every flyer he was offered and dropped them all dramatically. He paraded into another alley, this one darker.

I felt a furious worry that I did not want to feel for some-one like Manny.

"Slow down," I shouted.

Six women, clearly prostitutes, white, black, Asian, high-heeled up to him. He stopped. They touched his head, his shoulders, his hairy arms, his waist. In English they praised his Czech. They picked his pockets.

I caught up. Four of the women clopped my way, smiling, glittery and glossy, smelling of fruits and soft spices. I told them to go fuck their mothers.

One said, "You would like that?"

The others left in a casual hurry.

"Yes?" said the one still there.

Her expression had changed so gracefully that I couldn't remember what its meaning had been when directed at Manny. To me she was trusting, sincere.

I didn't work hard enough to look away.

Her face said, With you I can be myself.

Will you let me be myself?

Let me—

Her mouth opened. She stepped toward me.

I grabbed an unresisting Manny, who'd been grinning, and hauled him into walking away, saying, "They picked your pockets, are you stupid, check them, check your pockets."

When I was sure that the prostitute hadn't tailed us, I let go of Manny's shirt. We were the only two people in the alley, but I smelled a cigarette being lit, the special fragrance of a first drag. I stopped. I let myself imagine what it would be like to smoke a pack straight through. I let myself imagine smoking this pack straight through in the bedroom of my apartment, what had been T's and my apartment, sharing cigarettes, using cigarettes to light more cigarettes, the hot smoke curling out of our mouths and into our clothes, our clothes coming off, our clothes off, T laughing, T touching my chest, T laying out the logistics of a trip we would take to California in which we would dodge the Chicago winter and rent a convertible with racing stripes and gun it on the 101 to beaches and mountains and cities and campsites while listening to show tunes she'd make me sing along to, You will sing, she sang to me, You will sing sing sing, she sang, pulling me into her and gasping. I gasped.

Manny was staring at me.

His condescending smile had been bent by pity. The pity was for me.

I shouldered him like he was a door I needed down. He staggered from the hit, stunned. I stepped up and shoved him and he fell on his ass. His glasses stayed where they were exactly. It took more than it should have to stop myself from kicking him in the side of the head.

"There is nothing in my pockets!" he screamed. "I left my wallet at the apartment on purpose!" he screamed. "You are a fuck!" he screamed.

We walked to the apartment on main streets, our positions reversed. He muttered insults at my back, revising them.

"Cretin."

"Cretinous thug."

"Cretinous neanderthug."

At the door to the apartment I struggled with the lock. It required force and concentration. I paused to refocus, to better ignore Manny, and noticed that the rows of door buzzers were all labeled with the same name: mine. Only the slot next to my apartment number was blank, an empty space.

"Stanley," said Manny as I unlocked the door, his voice warped. My name rolled off his tongue like a square.

I opened the door.

"Look," he said, pointing down.

Stanley Reluctantly Observes the First Figure, Which, for Reasons That Aren't Clear to Him, Reminds Him of Barton

A chalk drawing: the life-sized outline of a body, as seen in old detective films.

Depicted as if collapsed across the threshold, the arms in the lobby, the legs in the alley. The proportions realistic. A man of under-average height and slim build, on his side.

Stanley and Manny Enter the Apartment Building

Manny squatted and touched the lines that suggested the head. "I believe that this is chalk," he said, trying to muffle his fear.

I stepped over him, whacking his arm on accident, and took the noisy stairs thinking that if I saw the made-up man I'd hook him into a headlock and crush him unconscious and hurl him down the stairs with a murderous howl. I felt afraid of myself. This fear, I'm ashamed to say, made me proud.

"It is chalk," shouted Manny from below.

I walked the hall to the apartment, passing the lantern-style fixtures that cast overlapping cones of dusty light. The ones nearest the door were out.

Stanley Reluctantly Observes the Second Figure, Which, for Reasons That Aren't Clear to Him, Reminds Him of Torrentelli

A chalk drawing: the life-sized outline of a body, as seen in old detective films.

Depicted as if on its stomach, reaching for the apartment door. The proportions realistic. A woman of average height, one arm crossing the threshold of the door and disappearing into the apartment.

Stanley Enters the Apartment

I unlocked and opened the door without looking at the rest of the second figure and saw a large purse on the kitchen table. It could accommodate two skulls. I pulled a beer from the fridge, a pilsner, and sat on the couch. The couch was silent.

"This figure is meant to be holding a purse," said Manny, bent by the door. He stood up. "There is the purse."

I searched for the remote.

Manny clapped at me, as if seeking the attention of a pet.

"Do not think that I agreed to stay in this apartment without knowing that it would become the epicenter of a pretentious work of performance art. But do not think that my decision in any way absolves you of responsibility, Stanley."

I turned on the TV. Four stations, four species of static.

Manny marched over, holding the purse the way you'd hold a dead thing by the tail. He dropped it on the coffee table. Its skinny lip was snap-buttoned shut. "*Your* uncle!" he said. "*Your* arrangements! *Your* predicament, whatever it may be, is placing *me*—and possibly others!—in a predicament. Open this purse!"

I turned off the TV and looked at him.

He smacked the beer out of my hand. It gurgled and spluttered on the floor.

I said that if he hit anything out of my hand again I'd punch him right the fuck in the face.

He tapped the lip of the purse, an order. He wasn't afraid of me but he was afraid.

I snatched it up. What was in it was hard and heavy. I walked to the window, opened the screen, took two steps back, wound up, and shot-putted the purse straight out. It slapped onto a roof across the street.

"I'll take the couch," I said, taking the couch.

Manny, incredulous, declared that he'd be gone in the morning.

He slammed the bedroom door—it bounced open, spitting flecks of paint. The frame was swollen. He wrestled the door as closed as he could, hissing, then huffed into the bed, which was as squeaky as the stairs.

I sat up to shut the window. Then I walked to the open door and stood in the hall. The lights by my doorway, which had been off, were stuttering on. No sounds of any sort mumbled or bumped from the other units on the floor. The silence felt enforced—in it was the sense of men behind doors, holding their breath, waiting for signals.

I closed the door to my apartment nearly all the way and set the beer bottle on top.

From the bedroom, a cell phone tinkled. Manny groaned.

I went to my laptop, which was where I'd left it, folded shut on the coffee table. It had been given its own chalk outline. Under the fluorescent light the chalk had a dim shine, a ceremonial glow. I hesitated. I didn't want to open my laptop if doing so meant collaboration with my uncle's project, but I didn't want to keep my laptop closed if doing so meant the betrayal of my principles of self-protection. I wanted to refuse to cooperate and I wanted to refuse to allow my actions to be influenced. I wanted total untouchability. I was drunk. I said to myself, Which of the available actions is the action that is the most "me," which was something I hadn't said to myself since high school, when I said it daily, when it served me in a way I didn't understand—when it led me to believe in a self that was true, a self-aware self, honest and genuine, achievable by honest, genuine, and self-aware actions, even as I simultaneously believed in its opposite, the presented self, every action false, every self a conscious or subconscious "act"—and in thinking these thoughts thought left me and I was lifting the laptop out of its outline and I was opening it and I was sitting on the couch. The background had changed again: a black-and-white picture of me from behind, in Prague, crossing a street, headed for the hard darkness of an alley. I looked like I was on my way to commit a crime. No email from T. One email from my brother titled, "Tip #4: Shadow Puppet Sex Show!" and then another titled, "Tip #5: Anti-Hangover Garlic Soup, a Czech Tradition" and then another titled, "Mom's in Krakow!" and then another with no subject, and then another titled, "You and T broke up?"

One from my aunt: "Fly home now."

One from myself, from my email account to my email account, from Stanley to Stanley, sent not by me but by my uncle or an artist who had opened my laptop or otherwise accessed my account: "COMPLETE EXPLANATION OF THE MADE-UP MAN."

I deleted them all unread. I wrote an email to T, saying, Manny's here now and I hope you enjoyed the play you saw tonight and also the dinner and break a leg see you tomorrow let me know where you want to meet and when, I'm sorry I didn't bring my phone I thought it'd be easier to stick to my plan without out a phone, I wanted to be unreachable, but now I regret it I have to rely on email will you email me when you want I'll check in the morning. I reread for typos. I wrote, "I miss you." I changed it to "Miss you." I deleted it. I wrote "Miss you" again and I sent it.

Several kinds of terrible entangled me. I would not be tripped into regret, I said to myself. I would be a man who could move out of anything. A trap. The truth. Himself.

Behind my back, in the bedroom, Manny sighed with hatred.

It was possible that I was thinking out loud. I didn't want to. I didn't want to participate in any way.

I closed my laptop and returned it to its chalk outline.

I removed the bottle booby-trap and closed and locked the door. On the couch I chugged what was left of the foamy slop. I tucked the bottle under my arm.

Sleep shoveled onto me.

I squirmed in a dream in which I encountered the space at the center of myself that wasn't me. The space was made up of a form of matter so unstable that it was impossible to make a study of it just by being near it once. I touched its surface; my hand stuck. Space, I said, not moving my mouth, how are you in me but not me. Every window in a city broke. I stood on a street in which a bad thing had happened many times. I stood in a white river, and it crested, and then it was the white river that stood in me, and I crested. I tore an alley down into itself. My hand broke off at the wrist.

I woke to knocking.

"Okay," I said, getting up, "yes."

I pissed in the toilet. Manny's little bag of toiletries, open, sat on the tank. Every product in it was Italian. The clock read 3:00 a.m.

The knocking continued.

I squinted through the peephole. In the hall stood the made-up man. He wore a dress.

He said, "I saw your mother."

I bumbled back to the couch.

A key scratched in the lock. I sat up.

The door opened. "I am your friend," said the man.

I was wrong—he wore a high-waisted skirt and a high-neckline top, both pieces tight, black with white patterning. His long dark hair spilled from an unraveling updo. He smiled, uncertain. It occurred to me that this might not be the middle-aged man from the airport and the train station, that this might instead be a young woman whose face had been made up to resemble his made-up face.

"I know you," he or she said, nodding.

I said nothing.

He or she spoke in the voice of a woman impersonating a man impersonating a woman.

"I have forgotten. My purse. I have forgotten my purse."

I said that I'd thrown a purse out the window.

He or she put a hand to his or her chest and, with a worried look, said, "I do not feel safe."

This person, I realized, was a twenty-something woman made up to look like a fifty-something man made up to half-look like a woman.

"Please leave," I said in an unfriendly way.

"I will tell you the truth," she said. "If I will tell you the truth, you will tell yourself the truth. If you will tell yourself the truth, you will tell the truth to family. You will tell the truth to friends. You will tell the truth to strangers."

She started to cry.

"I do not actually know you," she said.

I approached her in an unfriendly way.

She backed into the hall, as if frightened, and stepped on an overstuffed envelope, a new one. She glanced at it and then at me. I felt sorry for her and tricked by her, I wanted to help her and I wanted to terrify her. I was rattled by how much she'd rattled me.

She pointed at the envelope. "Is it for you?"

I closed the door and locked it and wedged a chair in front of it and returned to the couch.

She was whispering, "I do not feel safe."

I didn't think that I could fall asleep to that.

A little after eleven in the morning I woke to Manny moaning.

I went to his open door. He lay beside the bed on an improvised mattress of folded clothes and luggage, including my luggage. He held his forehead like it had a leak.

"That unsuitable mattress. Has triggered. A mid-level migraine."

He'd made the bed. On the pillow sat a single dress shoe, a scuffed-up loafer. It had the look of a piece of evidence.

I fetched a glass of water for Manny and put it on the floor.

He was pale and tense, tight in a state of careful self-containment. It seemed to hurt him to keep his eyes shut.

I wanted to leave the room but didn't.

Stanley Remembers His Mother's Migraines

Sit here, she'd say.

I'd sit at her feet at the end of the couch.

But don't speak, all right?

I wouldn't: I was a boy who listened.

Thank you, Stannyfanny.

I'd watch her face and worry. She'd lie there, rigidly re-laxed, a hand on her eyes. I'd see hot lines etched inside her head—searing rows, searing columns—and it wouldn't be long before I'd sympathized myself into my own minor headache, a dull wobble.

I'd put my hand on my eyes. The wobble would drag—it would scritch.

One time I asked how come headaches were contagious.

She smiled. Try to think less.

Stanley Remembers a Time When He Tried to Think Less

I stood in line to board the plane to Prague.
    I stayed in line.
    I boarded the plane.

Stanley Remembers Another Time When He Tried to Think Less

"Abbey's got it made," said my mom. "Be happy for her. For once."

"Are you this stupid on purpose?" said my dad.

My mom and my dad had taken me out to an early dinner at Starpolska. We were the only customers there, seated in the middle of the main room, waiting for our pints of Polish beer to appear. It was my birthday.

This was at a time when my mom and my dad were seeing each other again but pretending they weren't.

This was right before Ro.

My brother had texted: he'd be late.

"Stanley, honey," said my mom. "Do me a favor. Imagine you're in your late thirties. You've been dating a bunch of kooks. The problem with the kooks is that they start off seeming really interesting, because of their kookiness, but after a week, they're boring. They were boring all along. You're getting pretty tired of it. Your brother's bugging you, trying to get you to date somebody with a 'serious' job. You're just about to give up, maybe even leave the country. Why not? But then, just by chance, you meet a *really special kook*. This kook is different from the others—this kook is just as crazy about archaeology as you are. Maybe even crazier! Next thing you know, you're seeing archaeology in a new way. You didn't think you could love archaeology any more than you already did, but there you are. And guess what? You start to love the kook, too."

"That's not it," said my dad.

"Plus the kook is rich," said my mom.

"No," said my dad. "No."

"Would you be happy? Would you want everybody to be happy for you, including your brother?"

My dad leaned forward. "Say you're with a girl you know you shouldn't be with."

"How do you 'know' that?" said my mom.

"The way she treats the people she works with is goddamn terrible."

"But they agree to it," said my mom.

"It's goddamn terrible," said my dad to me. "You know it's goddamn terrible, everybody knows it's goddamn terrible. And that's just part of it, that's just one red flag on a whole fucking highway to hell of red fucking flags. Because you know this, most of the time you're with her, you feel bad. But some of the time, for other reasons—the reasons that got you together in the first place—when you're with her, you feel good. Good enough to make it hard to go."

My mom and my dad didn't look at each other.

"What would you think," said my dad.

"Honestly," said my mom.

Stanley Almost Has a Realization

I sat on the "unsuitable" bed. Its springs wheezed.

Manny slurped at the water. "Tell me," he said. "Who exactly was here last night?"

I told him about the made-up woman, what she'd said, how she'd tried to lead me to another envelope, but I didn't give him the history of her appearance, how "she" had been a "he" at the airport and at Kutná Hora. I also didn't go into how something in her manner, something that had nothing to do with her appearance, had spooked me.

He was about to ask another question, then winced. He cooled his hand on the glass of water and applied his palm to his forehead.

I started to feel bad about having shouldered and shoved him.

He muttered, as if adding up a sum.

I asked him if he had any migraine medication.

"Ja, in Deutschland."

"I'll run out for some," I said. "I don't mind."

I didn't—it would be a relief to escape the apartment.

Manny picked up his phone, found a nearby pharmacy, and instructed me to hurry. If I didn't, he said, we'd miss our chance to get a table at Café Slavia, a sociohistorical must-see, onetime haven to eminent intellectual dissidents.

"I am obligated to repay you for last night's dinner," he explained.

I'd never known Manny to be obligated to anyone but T.

At this point, the picture began to come together.

Manny stared at me.

I said, "Why are you in this apartment."

His phone tinged.

His phone ting-tinged.

Stanley Has a Realization

T had persuaded Manny to stay with me.

Stanley Imagines How T Persuaded Manny to Stay with Him

1. T tells Manny about *Black and White and Dead All Over*'s acceptance into an internationally acclaimed theater festival in Prague.
2. Manny, impressed, insists on visiting from Berlin.
3. Before checking with me, T offers Manny lodging at my uncle's apartment. She talks up the location.

    When does anybody ever get to stay so close to Old Town Square, for *free*?
4. Manny, to whom only money is authentic, is tempted.

    If it were not for the roommate, I would find this agreeable . . .
5. T tells Manny about the art project.

    I'll be honest. If you were there to keep an eye on Stanley, even for just a day or two, I'd feel so much better about him being in the middle of this.

    I've told you about his uncle, haven't I?

    The wealthy and unethical artist?

    Whose "theme" is exploitation?

Stanley Almost Has Another Realization

Manny rolled the glass of water across his forehead.

"Numerous interests," he said. "Have necessitated my presence."

I picked up the dress shoe that'd been left on the bed and checked the size. It would fit my foot.

We were both in this apartment because of T.

We were both in this apartment because of who we wanted to be in relation to T.

We were both in this apartment because of who we thought we were or wanted to be or hoped we were in relation to T.

T in relation to that.

T in relation to her new roommates in a new apartment in Chicago, and T in relation to her old cast and crew in an old apartment in Prague.

T in relation to the stage.

T on a stage.

Manny put down the glass. He did what he could to conceal his irritation.

"What," I said.

He returned to texting, willing me to go.

"The café awaits," he said.

Stanley Has Another Realization

T was going to be at the café.

Stanley Imagines T at the Café

T sitting at a table in the café, looking like the subject of a photo, a photo fit for the café's wall.

T touching the handle of her untouched cup of coffee.

The people at the other tables thinking T is a famous person.

T knowing this about the people at the other tables but not thinking about it.

T thinking about us, about our break:

T imagining me imagining her:

T imagining me on my way to the café:

Stanley Controls Himself

When I could be sure that my voice would come out okay, I said, "What time is T getting to the café."

Manny lowered his phone to look me in the eye. "T will not be present."

Stanley Remembers the Last Time Manny Lied to Him

We were at the Half Acre Tap Room, T's favorite microbrewery, post-bowling. The place was jammed but we'd scored seats, our table wet with sloshed beers. Hip white kids in tight coats and colorful scarves crammed up to the bar. Music boomed. Every song sounded like an homage to the one before it.

Manny sipped his snifter of barley wine and made disappointed faces at his phone.

T and Inna stood in line for the bathroom right in front of me. Inna was shouting Russian words, and T was shouting them back. Even though I'd been with her all night, for dinner and bowling and drinks, an empty-house feeling popped and creaked inside me, the same empty-house feeling that popped and creaked when we'd go a week without seeing each other, which wasn't uncommon with her rehearsals and my classes and our part-time jobs.

Just the night before, on video chat, she'd suggested that we live together.

I said I was unsure about sharing the same space all day and all night.

She asked me if I was sure of her.

I was.

She'd made a gesture that said: Then what's the difference?

"Poshlost," shouted Inna.

"Poshlost," shouted T.

The line moved.

Manny sighed.

I asked him how long he and Inna had been boyfriend and girlfriend.

He lowered his phone to look me in the eye. "She is but a friend."

My first impulse, to respect his privacy, was undone by my second impulse, to disrespect him respectably.

I said, "Why do you talk like that, like you're from some other fucking century, the nineteenth century? 'But a friend.' 'Unto you.' 'Enabling feminine graces.'"

He considered my question.

Two skinny tattooed dudes wearing slightly different versions of the same stupid hat flirted with T and Inna. Through the short distance she seemed even smarter, even more surprising. Later that night, right before we went home to separate apartments, I would tell her this, and she would say it worked the same the other way around: she never loved me more than when she saw me from across a room.

At the time that wouldn't strike me as sad.

Manny said, "I know who I am, therefore, I can be who I like."

Knowing who you were didn't mean that you could change yourself whenever you wanted, I said, it meant the opposite. Manny interjected but I talked through him, saying that knowing who you were was like conducting archaeological research on long-gone cultures: you discovered a little at a time, you worked to figure out how it fit, you stepped back to study the big picture. You challenged the theories of respected experts. You were always on the lookout to update your understanding, knowing that there was a "next understanding" that was more complete than what came before it, a truth you ascended rungs of discovery to reach.

Manny nodded with insincere awe.

"How insightful!" he said. "And insecure!"

"You know who you are: a prick," I said. "You don't choose to be anything else."

He raised his snifter. "You're an idealist. You *can't* choose to be anything else."

Stanley Remembers Other Uncomfortable Assessments of His Character

On my first demolition job with Niko, I asked about the damaged insulation I'd be dismantling, when it'd been installed, what was in it. He handed me the mask, the goggles, the gloves. "Didn't know you'd be a smart one," he said, to which I said that a concern for safety didn't always signal intelligence, to which he whistled and said, "Wise, too."

The summer after my first year of college I met up with Torrentelli at the Art Institute. As we walked through the at-the-time-brand-new Modern Wing he told me that he'd be transitioning to a woman—I'd had no idea—the therapy and the hormones and the surgeries, everything, he'd change his name from Antonio to Serenity. We sat on a bench by his favorite Dubuffet. I was the first person he'd told other than his nonna. I didn't ask why, but he said, as if I had: "You're not judgmental."

One fall I helped Barton move from Rogers Park to Bridgeport during a surprise flood-watch thunderstorm. I was the only person he'd asked who showed. We ran through screens of rain, we loaded his car, we loaded my car, we chugged across swirling intersections and viaduct pop-up ponds. While we sat on the floor at his new place, which had lost electricity, drinking beers and waiting for the pizza to never arrive, he said, "You only did this so I'd owe you one."

One winter my college friend D-Mac dumped his long-term girlfriend again. I gave him a bottle of Bulleit and helped him drink it, and because he didn't want to talk, we played chess, backgammon, and Stratego, and I beat him at all three. He dug up a card game he used to play, Shadow Traveler, I'd never played, and after I beat him four or five times he slapped himself on the head and screamed, "Fuck *me*, you're that fucker who's good at every game he plays!"

At a year-end grad school party last December, Golnaz, my partner on a final project, gave me a hug. Then she gave me another one and said, "You're a softie."

"You're good to have around," said Dr. Madera.

"You know what you're doing," said my brother.

"You are representative of America," said my uncle, as I put the check in my pocket.

Last May, I told my mom over the phone that it'd be better if we didn't talk for a while. She laughed and said how long is a while. I said I would know it when I knew it. She said, "Manly Stanley being manly."

Stanley Remembers an Uncomfortable but Accurate Assessment of His Character

On a sticky June morning, T and T's actor friends and I moved all of T's things out of what was suddenly just my apartment and into a rental truck. The rental was too big—when we finished, more than half the trailer echoed, empty. I pointed out that T's stuff would slide around on the drive. The actor friends insisted that the last layer, a border of the heaviest boxes, would prevent that from happening, but I fetched bungee cords from my car and strapped all of T's things tight. Everyone else watched from the street, sweating. T tried to look neutral. Afiya, T's other oldest best friend, who'd come down from Milwaukee to help her move, cupped her mouth and said that what I was doing was not fucking necessary.

"Hello?" said Afiya.

On my way out I clanged the trailer door shut.

T and Afiya climbed in up front, T in the driver's seat. She waved me to her window.

Afiya rolled her eyes.

The keys were in, dinging, but T hadn't turned the engine on. She was wearing workout clothes, her big hair under a ball cap. She looked like a pop star trying not to look like a pop star.

"You don't have to help us unload," she said. "You've done so much already!"

I told her I didn't mind.

Afiya said, "Don't help us unload."

"I'm okay with it," I said to T.

T's face had set into a forced centeredness, a state of trying-not-to-cry. It didn't feel good to see it.

She said, "Most of the time, you don't know what you're doing, do you?"

"I'm waiting for you to cry," I said.

I was crying.

Afiya rolled up the window.

Afiya started the truck.

Afiya yelled.

T drove away—the truck coughed down Sunnyside, past old green trees and big houses with porches, through a yellow light, and onto Lincoln.

The actor friends followed, all five of them clown-carred in a two-door. They sang along to a peppy show tune. Every one of them looked at me and saluted.

Stanley Recalls How T Planned His Surprise Birthday Party

"T is attending other events!" said Manny, exasperated.

"In case you have forgotten," he said, "she has come to Prague to participate in a *festival*. Workshops, presentations, panels, spontaneous conversations. Followed by her own performance this evening. She does not have the time to appreciate a cup of kava with myself, you, or anyone else!"

I let him know by how I looked at him that I knew this was a lie.

He grumbled. "And even if she *did* profess to have the time to meet—I would not, under the current circumstances, permit it."

T would be at the café.

I stood up.

Manny's mood changed: he turned somber. He tucked away his phone.

"It is extremely important that you listen to what I say next," he said.

I saw straight through him. T had carved out the time to meet that afternoon; she hadn't emailed me about it because she wanted it to be a surprise; to better set up the surprise, she'd conscripted Manny, who was unwilling but obedient.

"I am going to ask you a question," said Manny.

T delighted in masterminding surprise schemes.

I thought of the many times she'd enlisted my help in pulling fast ones on her friends for their birthdays and bachelorette parties, how I'd provided diversions and delivered props, how I'd told strategic lies on her behalf.

Then I thought of the last time she'd tricked me: one week before my most recent birthday, she'd made me clear my schedule for it. "It's your day, but you are mine mine mine," she sang, hanging from my neck, naked, as I tromped from the bedroom to the kitchen, naked, to grind coffee. This was in March. We'd been living together in Lincoln Square for a month, and we were discovering that we weren't so bad at it. Nothing new and ugly emerged from chore division or cleanliness standardization or kitchen usage or bathroom sharing or sex frequency. My uncertainty about moving in together—an uncertainty that lost shape when I tried to explain it to her, but that firmed up, square and solid, when I was alone—seemed to be gone for good. We congratulated each other to sleep. It seemed like the celebration of my birthday would in some way be the celebration of living together successfully. The night before my birthday, a Friday, T returned from a late rehearsal angry at herself. She said she'd realized that she'd double-booked the day—months ago she'd committed to a trip to Milwaukee to visit Afiya, to help out with a staged reading of her new play. I insisted that it was fine. It was. T, as disappointed as she was determined, sat on the kitchen counter and punched at her phone. She proposed make-up dates, she searched for replacement activities, and in the time it took me to drink a pop, she'd bought tickets to a concert the next week. Although she didn't say who the act was outright, she hinted that we'd be front-row for Marilyn Manson, whom I'd followed in high school with intense devotion but could no longer listen to without wading into a reservoir of residual self-hating shittiness from that shit-rich stretch of my life. I couldn't tell if T was joking. She opened her arms—I hugged her off the counter. She smelled like rehearsal, sweaty and musty, and I loved it and she knew it, and she shook her hair in my face. She radiated such devious pleasure that I didn't push her with questions. The next morning, my twenty-ninth birthday, I woke to T having sex with me. We didn't check our voices and we didn't stop the headboard from applauding with the wall, and when I said that I was about to come, which I'd never said to her before, she shouted that she loved me, which she'd shouted before but never during sex, and she was crying, and so was I, and she reached for my face and covered my eyes, and I closed them under her hand, and in the darkness everything deepened. We dropped beyond our selves. We weren't even what we were doing; we were one wide dream. Then a bright fear flashed: what this happy weepy unembodied moment signaled was nothing more than the acknowledgment of the unlikeliness that our relationship would last. A moment of missing us before us became memory. I denied this fear. I said: Fear, you are only the feeling that I have when I cry. You are only the feeling that reveals the fact of my status as a product of a culture that teaches its men to undo any feeling that is not a feeling of strength or of comfort. I am a site of sociohistorical influences, I said, a backyard of buried trash and valuables that I am incapable of digging through objectively. I thought about the circumstances that allowed me to think these thoughts, the basic needs met, the lack of fear of oppression and suppression—I thought about my maleness, whiteness, lower-middle-classness—I thought about how I wouldn't be having these thoughts if it weren't for my aunt and Dr. Madera and T. We did not stop having sex. The bed jerked across the room beneath us. T took her hand off my face. She wasn't T—she was someone I might see on the L and wonder at, a woman I'd imagine futures with—I wasn't Stanley—I was someone she might see in the audience, between her lines and through the lights, a man that might as well be imaginary—then we kissed; we came; we were ourselves. I made eggs and kiszka for breakfast. T told an anecdote about a well-known acting teacher's controversial pedagogy. I carried her bag to her car.

She said that when we were married she wouldn't forget my birthday. I said that studies suggested that marriage degraded memory. She said that her own study suggested that by the time the two of us tied the knot, she'd have dementia. I didn't laugh. I wanted to, I couldn't—I resented that she'd told me a true thing. I resented that I couldn't make this true thing untrue. The moving in together was the thing that I could do and I'd done it, and despite everything going well with the living together I couldn't propose to her and mean it. I didn't know why: I didn't want to know why. T saw these feelings on my face. She got in the car, picked up an envelope, glanced at it, and handed it to me. Theater stuff, she said. Would I mind walking it to the mailbox right now to make the earlier pickup time, she'd planned to take it but the mailbox wasn't really on the way to Milwaukee. She honked out the first bar of "Happy Birthday" as she drove away. I went for a walk. Certain trees had budded, the smell of the soil had shifted. The tall couple with the snarly dog crossed the street to avoid me. Middle school kids played sixteen-inch softball at Welles Park while their parents watched, clapping and hooting. On Lincoln I passed restaurants and bars, banks and coffee shops. Couples spoke Spanish, German, Polish, Korean. Young musicians, carrying guitars and fiddles and banjos and basses, left classes at the Old Town School of Folk Music. I dropped the envelope in the mailbox and kept going, on to Western. Traffic had backed up already. I stopped at the liquor store for beer and cigarettes. Hassan, the owner, was surprised that I bought a pack, not papers and a pouch. I told him it was my birthday. He shook my hand and said, "I wish you every kind of health." I smoked two on the way to Welles Park, where I sat under a sprawling red maple and smoked two more. I tried to see the spring. Hidden squirrels wheeze-barked, trading warnings. Fat robins fought fat pigeons for trash-can overflow. A blasted-looking homeless man slumped along, not quite picking up his feet, his face damaged. When I was sure that sitting there wouldn't move me any closer to an understanding of myself, I headed home. On Sunnyside I passed an old church with a tall stained-glass window that my uncle had renovated last year. It depicted a Bible story I didn't recognize: men taking abstract actions in fields of concrete symbols. I wasn't familiar with common practice in the making of stained glass, but it looked like my uncle had used a lot of very small pieces where other artists might have used a smaller number of bigger pieces. The result was a steady, subtle warmth. Every section was in conversation with itself. I'd seen my uncle's windows in one or two other places, his renovations and originals, but until then I hadn't felt the effect of his enormously exacting patience. I crossed the street to our apartment. As I walked in the door, T and Torrentelli and Barton and six of T's friends (the five who would later help her move out, and Afiya) shouted, "Surprise!" Singing, they presented a cake decorated to look like the grid of a dig site. The frosting was dirt-colored and crosshatched, populated with Lego adventurer-archaeologists. One square had already been "excavated," cut away to show a filling packed with gummy skeletons.

My first dig, at the Cahokia Mounds State Historic Site, was a few months away.

That night at Huettenbar everyone laughed at me not only for having been to six Marilyn Manson concerts, but also for believing that T would take me to my seventh. Barton sauntered over to the internet jukebox and punched on the anthems from *Antichrist Superstar* and *Mechanical Animals*. Torrentelli bragged to Afiya about the trench coats and combat boots and piercings we'd had in high school, the dog collars and red contact lenses. She told the story about the parking lot fight, when Marcus Svachma and Ronan O'Kelly had been picking on her, when I fractured O'Kelly's jaw and knocked out one of Svachma's front teeth and Svachma broke my collarbone and O'Kelly stomped a concussion into my head. "For the rest of the year we called him Frankenstanley," said Torrentelli. Afiya regarded me with surprised respect, as if the fact that I'd been Goth improved me, or at the very least made me less boring. We all got drunk. The Marilyn Manson music raked across the edges of my happiness. From the other side of the room T threw devil signs and, between them, blew kisses. Barton tried to get Torrentelli to admit to having whacked off to whatever I'd written in her high school yearbook. Afiya handed me a pint and said, "I would have been friends with you." I gave her a side-hug.

"The Beautiful People" came on. T danced up to and around me, lip-synching, contorting her face through a slide-show of comically angsty sneers. I hooked her at the waist and drew her in. She pretended to lick my eyeballs. I asked her why she'd added the bit about the concert. "You must've known you had me," I said.

She picked up my hands and laid them on her face.

"I wanted you to think I didn't know who you were," she said.

53

Stanley Hears Artists in the Hallway

"Are you listening?" yelled Manny.

The air in the room felt newly stale.

I'd been sitting on the bed, saying nothing, and sweating.

I scratched at my beard. The smell of my body hit me: alcohol, airplane, pork-sweat. Being in an unfamiliar city, in an unfamiliar country, in a demented art project, in the company of a prick, in what I was hoping wouldn't play out to be the painful last act of a wrecked relationship—these five conditions, pulled like fingers into a fist, were punching me into myself, into memory.

The space at the center of myself that wasn't me still wasn't me.

Manny had started to pack his roller bag.

He said, "Am I in possession of your attention?"

He said, "To what degree do you believe your uncle to be *authentically* dangerous?"

The sooner I returned with his migraine medicine, the sooner we'd leave for the café, the sooner I'd see T. T was why I was in the apartment.

I was in the apartment.

"My uncle is a fake," I said.

"His resources are not 'a fake,'" said Manny. "His persistence is not 'a fake.' The ambition of his aesthetically juvenile project—to evoke the atmosphere of a supposed 'crime narrative' for no other purpose than to sabotage your sense of security and disrupt the lives of uninvolved individuals—several of whom, it must be said, have far more at stake than *you*—is not 'a fake'!"

I understood. "You think you're here to protect T," I said.

Manny rolled his shirts and slacks into tight bundles. As he shuffled around, he gave off the smell of booze-sweat. What I was witnessing was not a migraine on a veteran, I realized, but a hangover on an amateur.

"If you mean that I would prefer for my dear friend to remain out of the range of avoidable danger, then yes," he said. "I am T's knight."

The sound of slow footsteps came complaining up the stairwell.

I sat still.

Manny, sitting in the bedroom doorway, turned to the hallway door. The way the sound rolled through, it might as well have been open.

The stairwell muttered.

He or she reached our floor.

He or she, in heels, strolled the hall.

He or she stopped close to but not at the door to the apartment.

"This is your mother," said a woman.

She wasn't.

She waited.

I did nothing; Manny did nothing.

She sighed.

"I am not here," she said.

She click-clacked back to the stairwell.

Then down the stairs, a squeaking exit.

Manny started to say something, but before he could finish the first word, another woman in the hallway said loudly, "I am not here."

She seemed to be standing right where the first woman had stood.

This woman, like the first, waited.

Then sighed.

Then walked away on heels.

Instead of taking the stairs, she opened a door.

"It is difficult," she said.

The door closed quietly.

I motioned to the hallway. "Fake."

Manny massaged his temples. The second woman had frightened him.

"You were going to say something," I said.

He rubbed his eyebrows, his forehead.

"It was going to be about your hangover," I said.

He glared at me. "T informed me of an Easter performance . . ."

54

Stanley Recounts an Easter at Uncle Lech and Aunt Abbey's

My brother and I helped my aunt put together tables for twenty. We set the plates, napkins, and silverware. We brought in platter after platter of food. Our father sat at the head by two grotesque hams. He carved them gravely, pausing to complain about the quality of the knife, saying he'd be better off with a chisel. Aunt Abbey reached into a watering can and offered him an icepick. He smirked, which meant that he wanted to laugh, but wouldn't.

We started eating, just the four of us.

Then the back door opened. In came the Achy-Breakies on a wildness of whooping and stomping and clapping and ballyhooing, all of them rushing to be the first to the table, all of them dressed as thrift-store approximations of cowboys and truckers and hillbillies and hoboes. They spilled themselves into their seats. They hit their personal fifths of whiskey, a brand called Jackpot. Aunt Abbey, interested, passed the bowls of sides and the ham platters. The artists served themselves. Every one of them was talking to him- or herself, fully committed to a one-way conversation. The dining room became a chamber of monologues, the voices overlapping, layering, crowding up. My father ate angrily. Next to him, a spray-tanned man stashed food in his overalls. My brother tried to talk to a fake-bearded man in a Roy Rogers T-shirt who was going through the pictures in a wallet, every image eaten by burn-holes. The man next to me yahooed—all of the artists interrupted themselves to yahoo back, their shouts one shout, miraculously harmonized. This head yahooer was Uncle Lech. He wore a filthy white cowboy hat and a filthy white western-wear shirt and filthy white chaps. His mustache, more massive than ever, shined like a dress boot. He monologued with virtuosic speed and variation, bending his voice through multiple accurate-sounding imitations of regional American accents. It was stunning. He recounted his childhood in Dead Man, Illinois, and Truck, Kentucky, and Rear End, Missouri, and Conjugal Visit, Tennessee, and how his mama ran off with a gang of other mamas to steal the devil from the government while his papa stayed home and cooked himself dead to feed the family but a lot of good that did what with his twelve brothers getting killed twelve ways on accident on account of bum farm equipment and his twelve sisters getting killed twelve ways on accident on account of bum school equipment not to mention the ninety-nine vehicles his ninety-nine dogs had been run over by in a day. He jumped onto his chair. "America bless God!" he screamed, and he raised his bottle like it was a spear. The artists raised theirs in a violence of cheering and clinking. Uncle Lech chugged; he coughed and spluttered—he dropped the bottle, it shattered—he covered his mouth with one hand, and with the other, drew a revolver. The barrel's red rim marked it as a replica. He sprinted outside. My brother, sitting by the window, hand-visored the glass to look out into the night. "He's a-puking," he reported. "He's a-pointing his gun at his puke." Five shots exploded—astoundingly loud, much louder than the artists had been—and everyone quieted. My father stood, holding the carving knife. My brother ducked. The revolver smashed through the window. It kicked across the table and hit the floor, spinning. The smell of gunpowder hacksawed through the smell of the hams.

"Blanks?" said my brother, hopeful. His shirt collar twinkled with glass.

Aunt Abbey grabbed the gun before my father did.

"Give it to me," he said, his voice shrill.

With their faces matched in fury, they'd never looked more related.

Instruments appeared, harmonicas and jaw harps, mandolins and banjos, a jug, a washboard. The artists played—a low, mellow, lonesome melody.

My father held out a hand. In his other he still gripped the knife. He mastered his voice: "Now."

She went to the broken window and listened to the yard.

"Or else," he said.

She left through the back door, opening the revolver as she went, emptying spent casings into her apron.

My father put down the knife. I saw him feel everyone's eyes on him—he straightened, but tightened—and I was overrun with guilt, not only for being a member of the audience, but for feeling bad for my father, for pitying his pathetic threats—"Now"—"Or else"—which he wouldn't follow through on, which he couldn't even make specific.

My brother nodded to the music.

"We don't have to stay," I said to my dad.

He picked the knife back up. He stared at it, like he couldn't remember what it was for. Then he stabbed it so savagely into the table that the blade snapped. It slashed a check mark across his palm. Blood wicked his face.

Stanley Hears Artists in the Hallway, Again

"My dad took a cab to the hospital," I said.

Manny layered his bundled shirts and slacks into his roller bag. "An incident, then, in which the audience suffered real injury."

"He did it to himself."

"And have your uncle and his artists executed dangerous acts against one *another*, as part of a performance?"

I said that it was possible that they had.

Manny demanded an example.

I asked him what example he had in mind.

There was commotion in the hall: panicked footsteps, heavy voices.

Manny leaned over to watch the door.

"Stanley!" shouted a man, worried.

"I want to tell you what I don't want to tell you!" shouted another man, farther away, furious.

One of them pounded the wall to a different unit.

One of them paced, stomping with every step.

"Where's Stanley?" said the worried man.

"Is Stanley there?" he said.

"What happened to Stanley?" he said.

"I want to hear you!" shouted the furious man. "I don't, I can't!"

Something ceramic shattered.

"I can't do what I want to do!"

Another sudden smash, bigger.

Footsteps crushed and kicked broken pieces.

"Okay, Stanley," said the worried man, at the end of the hall. "You are you; I am I. I am sorry."

He said something else.

It sounded like: "Let's talk."

"Be like me and don't be me!" screamed the furious man, close to the door.

He attacked the door with object after object, ceramic, glass, ceramic, busting them, the pieces spraying and scattering, and then he beat the door with what sounded like his fists and his feet, screaming scrambled words, his scrambled words becoming howls, his howls becoming croaks, his croaks becoming raw.

Then the rasp of his ruined voice.

Shredded breaths.

A cell phone rang, a default ringtone.

"Stanley," said the worried man.

A second cell phone rang. The ring the same.

"Not Stanley," said the worried man.

The two men crunched away.

Manny uncovered his ears.

I felt like I'd been placed in a vise.

The space at the center of myself that wasn't me began to change.

"Christmas Eve!" Manny said.

He'd been speaking, waving.

"A Christmas Eve performance!" he was saying.

"Injury to artists!" he was saying.

Stanley Remembers a Christmas Eve at Uncle Lech and Aunt Abbey's

All week the temperature had wavered into and out of the double-digit negatives, the air so cold that when you breathed it, it slapped your lungs and you lost your breath. At my aunt and uncle's, however, we found the temperature leaning hard into a very dry 90 degrees. The radiators hissed and clanged insanely. My father shoved his coat at my aunt and said, "What a waste."

"I suspect it has a purpose," she said.

He scoffed.

"There are purposes beyond utility, you know."

"Wasteful ones."

"The end point of all utility is waste."

"Beer!" said my brother, handing everyone a can from his twelve-case.

We sat down to one table set for the four of us. We ate cheesy potato pancakes and pork gołabki steamed in bacon grease, Busia's recipes. By the time we finished we were sweating, especially my father, who refused to take off his sweatshirt, under which, I was sure, he wore a long-sleeved shirt, a T-shirt, and an undershirt. He was the kind of man who kept his condo at 59 degrees. He believed that "the inside needs to match the outside"—that the transition from one environment to another, temperature-wise, should be as short and as close as you could stand it, whether winter or summer. It spared the body needless shock, he said.

He killed three beers in the time it took me to drink one.

When my aunt brought out makowiec and butter cookies and coffee, we heard the artists file in through the front door.

After the Easter episode, my dad had insisted that the artists be forever barred from all future family gatherings. My aunt couldn't arrange that—it was Lech's house, too—but she did promise to confine the artists to other areas of the house, to keep them away from the dining room. My dad didn't like this, but he agreed.

He never once threatened to not show up.

"Those dinners we always do," he said.

To my brother, this was a sign of our dad's fearsome love for his sister.

To me, this was our dad saying to Lech: You can't fuck up my family.

Either way it made us love him.

That night, the artists assembled in what sounded like the living room. A speech began, steady, measured. We couldn't make out the words, but it didn't take long to discover what they were up to: they were "filibustering" the bathroom, blocking it with their bodies, so that everyone had to relieve themselves outside in the cold and the wind, with the exception of my aunt, who they addressed as "The Speaker of the House" and let through. My father tried the bathroom upstairs. "Locked," he said when he returned, but by the way he sat down, he made it clear that he'd pissed all over something that belonged to Uncle Lech. My brother laughed so hard he had to push himself away from the table. My aunt changed the subject to the time Busia tasted my aunt's take on the family potato pancakes recipe, when Busia had spat it out into a napkin, said to my aunt, "You are a fraud," and hobbled to the kitchen to make her own batch. "No one can say that she lacked principles," said my aunt, happily. I studied the expression of pride on my father's face: it was forced, its edges tense. A vengeful piss meant that my father had been played by my uncle, manipulated into lowering himself to his level, a thing that to my knowledge had not happened until right then. I stood up to go outside. My brother followed. While other yards shined with Christmas lights, my aunt and uncle's had been decorated with campaign signs and miniature American flags. It was so windy that our piss-streams whipped and waved, so cold that the splashes iced. "I've never seen Dad this satisfied," said my brother, delighted.

This annoyed me. "He's ashamed of himself."

"No way!" he said. "Every man longs for the day when he can justifiably piss on someone else's valuables."

"I don't disagree, I just don't see it in this case. I don't see it in Dad."

"You're not looking closely enough, that's all."

"I'm looking very closely."

"At your wee-wee?"

"Yes."

"Stanwee is awways wooking vwewy cwosewee at his wee-wees."

We zipped up. I went with him into the hall to watch the artists. Not because I believed in his interpretation, but because my disappointment in my father was peaking and I didn't want to be near him until I could hide it. The artists all wore conservative black suits and skirts, their ties and blouses red, white, or blue. They stank, a fund-raiser-in-a-locker-room blend of armpits, crotches, deodorants, colognes, and perfumes, all of it fermenting in the jacked-up heat. Every face dribbled sweat. Uncle Lech stood at the center of his artists, his hair and mustache trim, styled. He filibustered about bootstraps: their available sizes, colors, material composition percentages, load-bearing capacities, production costs, profit margins. A man acting as aide continually handed Uncle Lech large bottles of water, which he gulped down. Others drank them too. The labels read DIET WATER and featured crisp images of obese bald eagles. The eagles came in several variations, but every design was an offensive anthropomorphic stereotype of race, religion, or subculture. The bottles were dropped when empty, and as a result, everyone stood and shuffled on crackling plastic, crunching the bottles, sending them skittering. A huge-sounding bell donged. Uncle Lech stopped. He solemnly requested water. It was given. As he drank, he pissed his pants—piss darkened his crotch, piss ran over his shoes, piss spattered the floor. He dropped his bottle. Everyone else immediately pissed their pants and dresses. The smell was instantaneous: foul, dizzying, animal. A chain of puddles and channels crossed the floor. Only one artist didn't follow through, a birdlike man with a face so boring that it was unforgettable. I recognized him but couldn't remember his solo acts. The other artists objected, calling him a terrorist, and commanded him to do his duty, to e pluribus unum. He raised his hand, as if taking an oath—his skinny forearms poked out of his sleeves, revealing a series of tattoos of portraits of early American presidents—and he said, weakly, "My American fellows," but was cut off—the artists closed in, their soaked clothes smack-smacking. They stripped him. When they stepped back he wore only a sleeveless T-shirt and American-flag boxers. The colors on the flag were in the wrong places. He walked out the front door and into the killer cold, barefoot.

There was a moment of what appeared to be unscripted disagreement.

A pair of artists moved for the door, their minds made up.

Lech stepped in their way. He pressed his back against the door.

One of the two artists, a squashed old man, put forward a

quiet plea, while the other, a very tall young woman, raised her voice in outrage. The conversation was in Polish.

Lech said nothing and stayed put.

The two artists turned around, made for the back door, and hurried out. Their wet footprints twinkled.

57

Stanley Tells Manny the Truth

I didn't retell the Christmas Eve incident to Manny—of all the stories about my family that T had told him, he knew this one the best.

"The artist's exile?!" he said.

"Into the elements?!" he said.

He was seething.

I said, "If it was real, it was dangerous. I don't know."

"You insist on ignorance!" said Manny.

He left the bedroom for the bathroom.

I was sitting on the bed, playing with the dress shoe.

My own head started to hurt, a dumb pinch down the middle. I thought about how Torrentelli had encountered the pissing politicians project at a gallery in Pilsen. It sounded similar to what T had said about *Country-Western Country*: a multimedia collage in the style of a museum exhibition, a code-numbered series of items that documented the "filibuster" through pictures, audio, cell-phone video, and artifacts, such as the customized water bottles, the piss-stained clothes, and a desktop computer containing "sensitive state secrets" that had been "compromised" (pissed on) by a "hostile agent." There were also fake newspaper articles profiling the "congress" members. Torrentelli had remembered reading one clipping from the *Chicago Tribune*, possibly real, that mentioned how a nearly naked man had been found on a Rogers Park side street, dead of exposure.

"Art is what we are!" chanted a woman in the hallway.

She was at the door.

The doorknob rattled.

"We are what we see when we re-see ourselves!"

A ring of keys jingled.

"Fly home now," whisper-yelled a second woman, next to the first.

"Re-see yourself!" said the first woman.

Keys chunked in the lock, one after another. None of them worked.

"Wait," said the first woman.

"I'm leaving," said the second, heartbroken.

"These are wrong."

"I'm leaving you."

"This is a mistake. These are mistakes."

"I'm leaving you now," she said.

She sounded terrified.

The floor in the hallway creaked.

"Is that you?" said the women at the same time.

There was a scuffle—the sound of broken bits of ceramics and glass—then the thump of a tackle, and a high scream.

Then an awful pause.

Then two high screams—one was sustained; the other stuttered and restarted, restarted and stuttered; both moved away, as if the women were dragged to the staircase, where the screams were snuffed out.

I'd been standing, holding the shoe like a hammer.

The space at the center of myself that wasn't me turned, surged, pushed.

Manny returned from the bathroom with his pouch of toiletries.

"My suspicions are confirmed," he said, remaining calm. "At best, we are participants."

"That's the one thing I'm not," I said.

"At worst: fellow artists."

I said that the only actions I'd taken had been to disengage from the project. I listed everyone and everything I'd ignored, including what I hadn't already told Manny: the made-up man at the airport with the picture of me on his sign, the made-up man at Kutná Hora with the picture of me on his newspaper, the sequence of pictures of me that'd been exhibited on the background of my laptop, the artist who had walked up the staircase and entered a unit and launched the coordinated opening and closing of doors, the first envelope, the mug shots in the first envelope, the buzzers in the lobby that'd all been labeled with my name except for one, the chalk outline of Barton, the chalk outline of Torrentelli, the planted purse, the chalk outline around my laptop, the email sent from my account to my account "by me," the made-up woman made up to resemble the made-up man, the second envelope, and just now, the artists in the hallway—the women who were meant to be my mother, the men who were meant to be my father, the women who were meant to be my aunt.

Manny locked his roller bag and sat on it. "But you are here."

"Not for this performance, I'm not."

"If not for a performance, then for what?"

My throat caught. "I'm here for T."

Manny put his glasses on—I hadn't noticed that they'd been off. "You are here for Stanley, Stanley."

I began to swerve unsafely away from myself.

"I am here for Manny," he said.

Through my swerving I saw myself: choked, ugly, false.

Being and becoming who I wasn't.

Not seeing it, not saying it.

Lies.

"T is here for T," said Manny.

"I proposed to T and she said no," I said. "She moved out

of our apartment. We're not broken up but we're on a break. I don't know why I'm here: I don't know why because I don't want to know why. I'm trying to want to know why. I'm trying to want to know why I'm doing what I'm doing."

Manny looked hurt. "T lived with you?"

I cracked him in the face with the heel of the shoe. He fell off his suitcase—his glasses clattered across the floor—he threw his hands up to cover his head. He didn't move and he didn't speak. I tried to speak—I made a sound I'd never made before, a crumpled shout, a strangled bark.

Manny kept his face covered.

I took big breaths to plunge my anger down. I put the shoe in front of Manny.

"The shoe does not belong to me," he said, carefully.

"I'm sorry," I said. "I'm leaving."

In the hall I saw crushed plates, bowls, mugs, and glasses. They matched sets from my mom's apartment and my dad's condo.

I saw the second envelope, labeled:

EVIDENCE: COMPLETE EXPLANATION OF THE MADE-UP MAN

On it was a realistically rendered pencil drawing of my face. I looked too mean and sad to have friends.

Behind me, down the hall, a door opened. The two men who were meant to be my father rushed out, dressed the same: short-sleeve polos, paint-stained jeans, faded White Sox ball caps. They were backlit, their faces shields of shadow.

"That's him," said one.

The other spat on the floor. "Don't talk to whoever that is."

"Stanley . . ." said the first one.

From behind them popped a camera flash.

I would be a man who could move out of anything: I went the other way, to the stairs.

"Help," said someone through a door as I passed it.

The stairs groaned.

Halfway to the ground floor, I stopped.

58

Stanley, Remembering How the Made-Up Woman Made Up to Resemble the Made-Up Man "Left" Her Purse in the Apartment, Recalls a Night with Torrentelli

Last March, a week before I moved in with T, Torrentelli picked me up for an afternoon at the gun range. It was the first time we'd hung out since she'd changed her name to Serenity, since she'd completed the major surgeries. She wore a trendy T-shirt, a skirt, and dressy black cowboy boots. Her car smelled like a hair salon. She leaned across the center console and kissed me on the cheek, plocking me with lipstick. Her face and hair had changed in significant ways, and she had breasts—her voice had risen, her posture had shifted—but she was the same high-energy person, a fidgeter, a storyteller.

"What do you think?" she said, fluttering her eyelashes.

To me, the way she looked said: I'm different. And the way she acted said: I'm the same. That's what I told her.

"Like usual, you're only half right," she said.

I asked her which half was right.

"The way I *previously* looked was 'different.' The way I look right now, this is me, this is 'the same.'"

We edged onto 90/94, windows down, music up. This was when she told me that she'd seen the Pilsen gallery's exhibition of my uncle's pissing politicians project. There'd been audio recordings in which my family and I could be heard talking while we ate. She'd heard me say, "Thanks a lot."

"If you didn't sign a waiver, you can sue the shit out of them," she said.

The lawyer she worked with the most did privacy.

We exited the expressway, took a hard left onto a frontage road, and pulled up to an indoor range in the suburbs, just outside the Cook County line. She waved to a nerdy man in camo behind the counter. We clapped on ear protection, shared a stall, and fired away, taking turns with her handguns—the high-capacity 9mm semiautomatic her mom had given her when she'd turned eighteen, and the chrome-plated .357 revolver she'd bought brand-new to celebrate her transition.

With a gun in her hands, she was focused, still, precise. Every target we ran back to examine proved how thoroughly she'd outshot me—her groupings were always in the inner rings. I only hit a bull's-eye once.

Afterwards we grabbed some sushi takeout and a twelve-case and went back to my apartment, where most of my things were packed for my move to Lincoln Square with T. We sat on the floor by the coffee table. I didn't bother to put the case in the fridge—we piled the empties on the table. The more we drank, the more Torrentelli talked about her transition, about how she'd been having the sincerely holy experience of guiding her body into who she was.

"This might sound fucked up," she said, "but I keep think-ing about Catholic school, how the priests said that if you be-lieved, and you behaved, you could feel the holy spirit during Mass. I always believed and I always behaved, and I could never feel it. I wanted to, I wanted to so badly. And now it's like I'm finally feeling that. It makes me want to go to church again! That's the fucked-up part."

"The body of Christ," I said, presenting her with another beer.

She chanted a raunchy "Our Father," the one that'd landed us in detention our freshman year.

"What do you want to know?" she said. "Ask me anything, seriously anything. Don't be PC."

I asked her if she felt like she was "performing female" or if she "really felt female."

She smiled at me like my question was cute. "I've been 'performing male' for so long that 'really feeling female,' at least for a little while, is going to *feel* like a performance, sure."

She noted that even born-female women felt unsure, sometimes, about whether or not they were "being real women."

"Do you feel like you're 'performing male,' or like you 'really feel male'?"

I thought about it. "Performing."

This surprised her.

"But you're so comfortable with who you are!" she said.

This surprised me.

I opened a beer for myself. Torrentelli was sitting in such a way that I could see her underwear, a triangular flag. "I don't perform with T," I said. "I can't. It's really great, and it's really frustrating."

Torrentelli gushed about T, about how she'd like to find someone exactly like her, only a man.

"'T' is for 'Truth'!" she said.

"Tell her I said that," she said.

We killed the case.

Sleepy pauses started to enter our conversation.

Torrentelli wobbled up to go—she gave me a long hug and thanked me for being her best friend. She tried to kiss me on the cheek, but caught my ear. She left.

I changed for bed, poured a glass of water, and sat on the couch. I felt uneasy. It had something to do with Torrentelli thinking I was comfortable with who I was, and something to do with me being her best friend and her not being mine. I had misrepresented myself.

I texted T: Thank you for knowing who I am.

She texted back: you're not so hard to know :)

No I don't think my friends know who I am but
you do.
i know you pretty well, but they've known you
longer. they know other stanleys, more
stanleys. a cast of stanleys!
No.
oh doll. what happened?

The door buzzed; it was Torrentelli.
"I forgot my purse!" she said through the speaker.
The purse was right there on the coffee table, somehow
unseen. I grabbed it and went downstairs. Torrentelli stood
outside on the stoop.
I saw in her face that I wasn't wearing a shirt.
"Still not used to those things," she said, meaning the purse.
I handed it over. She hesitated.
"Can I tell you something?"
I felt my face break into a blush.
"Don't worry, I don't want to be your girlfriend!" she said.
I told her that she'd misread my reaction, that I wasn't an-
ticipating a declaration of love. But it was a lie. She'd read me
right.
"I ran into your mom," she said.
A month ago, Torrentelli had worked a table at a College
of DuPage career fair. She represented her law firm, talking to
legal-minded students, and when her shift was up, she remembered that my mom taught there, in Languages. She hadn't
seen my mom in years, and certainly not since her transition.
Since grade school, Torrentelli had been the friend my mom
liked most. My mom had called her "Sweet Tony" and sometimes "Sweet-tonio." This continued through high school. Even
though Torrentelli's grades were much worse than mine, and
she spent every day of senior year stoned, my mom liked to say,
"Why can't you be sweet, like Sweet-tonio?"
On her way out, Torrentelli dropped by my mom's office,

just to see. My mom happened to be there, grading exercises, eating crackers and canned tuna.

"She didn't recognize me," said Torrentelli. "Which I'm used to. But when I told her who I was, she kind of got this thoughtful look. Then she said, 'Did you lose a bet?'"

This had really hurt. Torrentelli could have pretended to laugh it off—she could have walked away with nothing more than a wave goodbye—but she'd reoriented her life to honesty. Honest thoughts, honest actions. So she told my mom no, this was her.

If my mom was embarrassed, Torrentelli said, she didn't show it. She didn't apologize, she didn't offer a supportive statement. She said, "Does Stanley know?"

Torrentelli poked me on the chest. "Why didn't you tell her?"

"We don't talk to each other much."

"Why not?"

"We don't know how."

"Okay, but why did she think *you* didn't know?"

"She doesn't think I actually know how to have friends."

Torrentelli frowned. "I'm not the best person for advice on this—you know how things were for a while with me and my mom—but for Christ's sake, call the woman."

I said I should, yes.

"Tell her things! Tell her true things."

She slung her purse.

"Heavy, isn't it?" she said.

"Moms," I agreed. "They fucking made you."

"No, my purse, I'm talking about my purse!"

She unclasped it to show me why: a third handgun.

Her concealed-carry permit had been issued. This was news to me—I wouldn't have guessed that she'd apply for one, or even approve of the law.

"I don't want to forget what it's like to conceal important information about myself," she joked.

I asked if carrying a hidden gun made her feel safe.

Her smile went stale.

"No. I feel just as threatened. I feel just as afraid. 'Safety' has nothing to do with it."

"Then why do it," I said.

"Stanley, I have so many reasons. All of them are awful."

59

Stanley, Remembering the Shoe That Manny Left on the Bed, Recalls When Barton Lived with Him

After he came back from college out of state, Barton moved into my Edgewater apartment. He stayed for a year, then found his own place in Rogers Park, just one neighborhood away, where he lived until he moved to Bridgeport. When we shared the place, almost every night was a late one—we played video games and board games, we drank beer and smoked hand-rolled cigarettes, we binge-watched TV. We ripped on each other like we hadn't left high school. I don't know how it started, but a running prank emerged: we hid each other's shoes under each other's pillows. One of us would go to bed late, drunk, or high, and not notice that he'd slept on his shoe until the next day when he was on the way out and reached for half a pair. At that point, the victim would laugh. The prankster, from somewhere else in the apartment, would laugh back. We'd laugh at the fact that we were laughing, that we were laughing at our laughter, that one of us had tricked the other in the most predictable way, again.

After Barton moved to Bridgeport but well before T and I moved in together in Lincoln Square, I invited everyone over on a weeknight to watch a Bulls playoff game. T was just beginning to get to know Torrentelli and Barton. I cooked a gigantic pot of bigos, Busia's recipe, a stew that called for more meat than I ate in a month. We ate and drank and booed and cheered. At halftime, I argued that we weren't good enough to be in the playoffs, and Barton argued that being in the playoffs meant, by definition, that you were good enough to be in the playoffs, and I argued that that was the system, yes, but systems allowed for mistakes because systems were themselves mistakes, and Barton said, "Your approach to life is a mistake."

Torrentelli said to T, "They're going through a divorce."

"That's devastating," said T. "Please don't tell me they have kids?"

"Just two big babies," said Barton.

"We thought it would save our relationship," I said.

The Bulls lost but everybody left in a good mood.

In bed, T said, "Wait a minute, sit up."

She extracted a dirt-crusty workboot from under my pillow.

"How did you not notice that!"

Laughing, I explained the gag.

"I don't know why we do it."

"I do," she said.

"Lay it on me."

She yawned. "It's how you say, 'I love you.'"

In the apartment above us, a little boy cried out, scared. His parents thumped over to his bed.

"Poor kid," I said. "Every other night, bad dreams."

"Whatever you say, Mr. Stanley-Change-the-Subject."

I tried not to grin.

"When you're ready to say it," said T, "don't go saying it with some fucking shoe. Okay?"

"What if I just say: 'I love you, T.'"

"That'll do."

The parents upstairs thumped back to their own bed.

"I love you, T," I said.

She didn't say anything.

I touched her waist—she snored.

"You're faking it," I whispered.

More phony snoring.

I wrapped her up in a half-submission. Then I very slowly made like I was going to tickle her.

She squealed and thrashed.

I held her tight and tickled her hard.

"I give up, I give up!" she said. "I love you too!"

Stanley Stops to Think

I sat on the stairs. Footsteps clattered into the hallway above me, a rickety cascade.

Manny said what might have been, "Get out!"

Stanley, Remembering Manny's Questions About Uncle Lech, Recalls Leaving His Aunt's Birthday Party Last July

Our dad and my brother and I stood in the backyard, finishing beers. We were almost drunk. The sun had dropped behind the neighbors' houses—it was too dark to play bags. My aunt, who hadn't said a word to me since telling me she'd talked to T, had darted inside as soon as I'd come back out, and we hadn't seen her since. It wasn't unusual for her to disappear near the end of a party, even if the party was for her. At any moment, my dad or my brother or I would say, "What time is it," and we'd leave, and it wouldn't be until my brother's birthday in October that the three of us would be in the same place at the same time again.

Music flipped on inside the workshop-garage, a distorted symphonic theme. Then off.

My brother said, "Want to do the crosstown classic next week?"

Our dad made indifferent sounds, I made indifferent gestures.

"I think I can get free tickets from my boss . . . ?" said my brother.

Right then, Uncle Lech popped out of the garage, closing the side door behind him quickly. Last I'd seen him, he'd been in the kitchen, pouring himself another double from the bottle of Chopin I'd bought for my aunt. He wore the same suit, only he'd swapped his black tie for a white one. He clutched a stout leather briefcase.

He eyed us like we were informants he had no choice but to trust.

I hadn't told my dad or my brother that an hour ago I'd agreed to apartment-sit for him in Prague.

"That man is a coward," said our dad, loudly.

Uncle Lech strode over. His warm and saintly expression from earlier, when he'd offered his proposal, had burned down to a business-only scowl.

He shoved the briefcase into my arms.

"Open in private," he said, his voice low and firm. "It is actual."

"Give it back to him," said my dad.

My brother connected a few of the dots: "Stanley got a Lech proposal?"

Uncle Lech walked back to the side door of the garage and knocked three times, with a flourish between each knock, as if enacting a secret sequence. He was let in.

"Give me that goddamn fucking thing," said my dad.

I took the briefcase to the overloaded garbage cans at the side of the house and crammed it into the least-crowded one. Only after I forced the lid back on did I notice that the briefcase had been oozing what looked like blood.

I turned to my dad and my brother. They hadn't seen the leakage.

"Do you know how he gets those desperate fucks from Poland to work for him?" said my dad.

I didn't.

"Do you know what he holds over their goddamn heads?"

I didn't.

"You tell him no," he said.

He was exhausted.

"I'll text you guys about the game," said my brother.

On my walk to the bus stop, I paused under a streetlight—

my shirt was smeared, but because the fabric was dark, the blood or fake blood didn't show much. I sniffed at one of the stains.

A drunk middle-aged woman in Cubs gear sat next to me on the brightly lit bus.

"You need me to call somebody?" she said.

I said it wasn't what it looked like.

"Your face," she said, stopping herself from touching me.

I checked my reflection in the window—a big bloody mark curved from my eyebrow to my cheek.

"It's fake," I said.

The woman nodded. "Then why are you so scared?"

Stanley Continues

I stood, unsteady.
    A woman with a deep voice spoke calmly to Manny.
    She may have been singing.
    I didn't go back up—I went down.

Stanley Resists Several Thoughts

It wasn't "getting personal." It'd been personal from the beginning.

It wasn't "getting real" because it was only going to get more faked, more staged, more set up.

It wasn't "getting out of hand" because I had a grip on it.

I wasn't in over my head.

Stanley Falls Down the Stairs

I tripped on the last flight and fell—I rolled, I banged my arms,
I banged my legs—

Stanley Encounters Two More Artists

—I stumbled out into the alley, I leaned against the wall. I panted. There was no other way to see it: T had supplied the anecdotes about Torrentelli and Barton that had been transformed into the performances I'd witnessed. Either she'd given the information to my aunt, during the post-show drink when she'd explained the state of our relationship, or she'd given the information directly to my uncle, when he'd approached her about playing a role in the project. Either she gave the information knowing what the consequences would be, and was okay with it, or she didn't know what the consequences would be, or was deceived, or didn't think it mattered.

A few floors in me had collapsed.

The space at the center of myself that wasn't me was splitting open.

I remembered T's texts: "I said no."

I remembered my aunt's face: I'm sorry I'm not sorry.

I walked down the alley and into a wind with no freshness, no smell of summer's end. Under the busted archway where the street began stood two men. One was big and bearded, in a black T-shirt and dark jeans. Even from a distance, he looked sullen, waiting with the cartoon surliness of an action movie goon. In front of him crouched a lean man in a suit and tie.

He took video of the big man with his phone, shuffling from side to side.

Each pretended not to know that the other knew that they were there.

The lean man, anxious, adjusted a setting on his phone.

The big man rubbed at his face like he wanted to wipe it off.

Stanley Has Three Realizations

The lean man, who had a mustache, was meant to be my uncle.

The big man, who rubbed at his face how I rubbed at my face, was meant to be me.

Me, myself, I, who stared at the men, stopped. I wanted to break their heads. Not out of any principle of self-protection, as I'd been insisting to myself, but only for the simplifying effect that another act of violence would have on me, however momentary, however false.

Stanley Deceives Himself

From the beginning, there'd been two choices:

Stanley Deceives Himself About His Strategy

to acknowledge or to not acknowledge the art project. Either choice, when made, subdivided into passive or active categories, combinations of action and inaction, avoidance and engagement. The line between "acknowledge" and "don't acknowledge" wasn't and wouldn't be clean, I knew that, but after I accepted my uncle's check, I decided to commit to an overall strategy of non-acknowledgment. It seemed to be the best way to stay simple. Even when things went bananas, I was sure I'd be able to hold close to "passive" and "avoidance." But in practice,

Stanley Justifies a Shift in His Strategy

in Prague, I'd found myself with no choice but to tilt toward "active" and "engagement." To be passive I needed to be active; to avoid I needed to engage. I hoped that these short-term concessions to acknowledgment would result in a greater degree of long-term non-acknowledgment. I was familiar with this strategy:

Stanley Critiques His Strategy

it was my father's. He'd used it steadily, with varying inflections and intensities, on Busia and my mom and my brother and me. It was not a strategy that worked. Sustained non-acknowledgment, at its heart, was sustained acknowledgment. As Manny had said, I was here.

They were there:

Stanley Is "Followed"

I approached the men who were in my way.

The man who was meant to be me set off into the street, as if he'd spotted someone he intended to hurt, and the man who was meant to be my uncle stayed ahead of him, facing him, capturing shots that would feature me in the background. They slowed at intersections, to wait for me to catch up a little, then turned one way or the other, guessing at which direction I'd go. Every time, they guessed right. They were "following" me in front of me.

When we hit the Square, they disappeared. Crowds teemed at restaurants and monuments and cafés, on the cobblestones and curbs, in the deep draws of shadow spilled by historic buildings. Couples crushed together for selfies. Tourists ringed chattering guides. The biggest gathering was massed at the clock tower, an assembly of families from around the world, standing, waiting for an on-the-hour cuckoo show. Noon was near. Hot smells from street stands cramped me with hunger: if I didn't eat, I'd puke. I veered to the end of a line for a fried cheese sandwich. I thought of the emails from my brother and my aunt that I'd deleted, unread. I thought of how anything anyone had ever emailed me and anything I'd ever emailed anyone could appear in some form in the project. The food-stand clerk, a young woman, gave me the two sandwiches and one bottle of beer I'd ordered. Her cheery smile surprised me. "Dziękuję," I said, and when I realized that I'd said it in Polish instead of in Czech, I corrected myself: "Děkuji." "Proszę," she said, and then, with a playful wink, "Prosím." She turned to the next customer. I stood there for longer than I should have, wanting her to smile at me again. On my way to find a place to sit, I passed the man who was meant to be me, standing in the line I'd just been in, with the man who was meant to be my uncle hovering at his side, out of line, filming him. The man who was meant to be my uncle, I noticed, was the made-up man from the airport. Amused tourists snapped pictures of them. "I bet they're doing a documentary," said a teenage boy. "Boring!" said a teenage girl. I sat on a curb with a view of the clock tower. The sandwich, a hot square of breaded cheese on a sesame-seed bun, gooey with mayo, was as delicious as my brother said. It steadied me. What my brother did was treat me like someone I wasn't. If he treated me like that someone, he seemed to think, then I might treat myself like that some-one, and if I treated myself like that someone often enough, I might become that someone. He'd learned this approach from our mother, a professor. It was a strategy of selective non-acknowledgment supported by a strategy of selective acknowl-edgment. To make your students smarter, our mother said, talk to them like they're smarter than they are. A young woman offered me a flyer for an orchestra performance, and another young woman offered me a discounted walking tour of "Kafka's Prague," and a young man offered me a coupon for a strip club, and another young man offered me cocaine. I unwrapped and ate the second sandwich, the one I'd bought for Manny. A young woman, in passing, let a flyer fall into my lap. It read:

ARCHAEOLOGY!
ARCHAEOLOGY . . .
ARCHAEOLOGY?

and included, parallel to the words, a column of three photos of my face. The photos were the same, but had been scrubbed with different effects, one scratchy, one bleary, one muddy. I couldn't tell where the source photo was from: I was beaming. I was damn happy. I watched the wind lift the flyer away. Noon struck—the crowd quickened—bells began to clang, slow and calm, trolley like. Four painted figures, attached to the clock tower's columns, shook their allegorical objects: a dandy and his mirror, a miser and his money bag, a turbaned man and his lute, a robed skeleton and its hourglass and bell. Higher up, on a stage, two windows opened to show a procession of serious-faced saints. They shuffled along like toys being made to walk by kids.

Phones and cameras rose in front of faces. Adults laughed, children shouted.

The bells stopped. The figures froze. The windows shut.

Just before the crowd broke, a handsome man, maybe in his thirties, dropped to one knee and proposed to a gorgeous woman, maybe in her twenties, right in front of me.

Stanley Is Embarrassed

The last proposal I'd been to was mine. We were walking on a beach by the lake, a timeout from a weeklong fight. T stopped to squint into a hot blue wind. No clouds, no waves, the skyscrapers molten with sunlight. T didn't look like a famous person or a person in a famous moment. My hands were in my pockets. We weren't sure I'd do it.

Do it, I said to myself.

Myself said: Don't.

I did—I took out the box, I took out the ring, I went to one knee—I vanished—no thought, no feeling, no body—a blast of unbeing—an on-and-on, an on-and-on-ing—until T said, "We can't."

"We can't," she said again.

Her voice was hollow wood.

I printed back onto myself, not on one knee, but on both. Before her as before the Mass.

Stanley Encounters Uncle Lech, the Made-Up Woman, and the Police

The handsome man looked as if he'd vanished from himself. The gorgeous woman winced.

Surprise and silence met in the faces of the crowd.

The man, on one knee, went down to both.

I lost my breath: the man was my uncle, the woman was the made-up woman. He'd been made up to look younger, and had cut his hair and shaved off his mustache, and she'd lost the middle-aged-man makeup, and had curled her hair. They were dressed for an evening out.

She said what sounded like, "We can't."

He didn't seem to hear it.

She said it again.

He heard it—he sat down, like I had.

"No!" said someone.

A horrible sensation occurred inside me. Everything beneath me flared and ashed and smoked, just out of sight, and everything above me whirled and sparked, just out of sight. I watched what was in front of me.

The woman helped my uncle to his feet.

He seemed weak, stunned.

She patted his arm and said something.

His daze broke—he jerked away, raising his hand to hit her.

He was going to hit her.

Then he dropped the role. His posture changed; he lowered his hand; he looked at me.

The look said: This is helping you.

Someone touched me on the shoulder. It was the man who was meant to be me, looking devastated. He'd been the one who'd said, "No!" He leaned in to whisper to me. I backed up, set a stance, and smashed him in the face with a right cross. He dropped.

The crowd rippled, covering my uncle.

There were shouts.

I pushed toward where my uncle had been.

A pair of plainclothes cops slammed me to the cobblestones. They cuffed me and hauled me to my feet. A third cop attended to the big man, who was sitting up. He'd vomited on himself.

I was shoved into a squad car.

The car took off.

My eyes pulsed.

The cop in the passenger seat swiveled around. He was about my age. He looked at me with interest and respect.

He said, "You are from where?"

Stanley Corrects His Observation

He looked at me with disgust. His disgust surprised him.

Stanley Corrects His Observation

He looked at me with what presented itself as a professionally impersonal expression, but not professional or impersonal enough to conceal his insecurity with the English language, which he didn't want to speak, but spoke.

Stanley Corrects His Observation

He looked at me like I was why he would quit his job.

Stanley Corrects His Observation

He looked like a grown-up version of a kid I'd gone to grade school with, an unsure and unhappy boy who'd been my best friend for a year, whose name I'd forgotten, who'd moved to LA. The last time we played together we'd gathered up our least favorite action figures and buried them in his sandbox, a secret parting gift, we agreed, to whoever moved there next.

Stanley Corrects His Observation

He looked at me and didn't look like anyone I knew.

Stanley Corrects His Observation

He looked at me and didn't look like anyone I'd known.

Stanley Corrects His Observation

He looked at me. I looked at him. I thought that I could read his face, but I couldn't.

Stanley Corrects His Observation

In his look, I saw myself looking at him, and in looking at myself looking at him, I saw that I'd been reading faces wrong. I tried to speak—horror winched me silent. I'd been seeing expressions, and from those expressions, assuming thoughts and feelings, and from those thoughts and feelings, assuming conclusions. My conclusions were inventions. I saw myself seeing T's faces, real and imagined, wrong. I saw myself seeing the faces of my brother and my aunt and my dad and my mom and Busia wrong. I saw myself seeing the faces of my uncle wrong. I saw myself seeing the faces of Torrentelli and Barton wrong, and the faces of Manny and the made-up man and the made-up woman wrong, and the faces of the fashionable old woman and the young mother and the young mother's kid and the attractive couple and the grim dad and the grim girls and the convenience-store clerk and the prostitutes and the prostitute who propositioned me wrong, and the faces of the women who were meant to be my mother and the men who were meant to be my father and the women who were meant to be my aunt and the man who was meant to be my uncle and the man who was meant to be me wrong, and the faces of the food-stand clerk, her too, wrong, and now the cop in the front seat, looking at me, his faces, wrong, and in his faces these faces, and in these faces mine.

Every mirror in me broke.

The cop said, "You are from where?"

PART II

NOT MY CIRCUS,
NOT MY MONKEYS

Stanley, in Jail, with Himself—

The space at the center of myself that wasn't me was now me.
Myself said: You.
I wasn't.
Myself said: Sleep.
I didn't.
Myself said: Think.
I did.
Sit up.
Stand up.
Puke.
Stop—sit, remember.
I was remembering myself.
I was remembering myself remembering myself.
I was remembering memory, or imagining memory, or remembering imagining.
I was saying, "You are from where?"
"You are from where."
"You."
"Where?"
Turn the tap.
Rinse.
Drink.
Turn the tap.

Dig.

I was from the dig.

The dig was bad but understandable.

The dig was a box I'd been in. It had stayed a box. I remembered its volume, its seams, its feel and smell. I knew who I'd been when I was in it. It was a "where" with a "you." Myself was there.

I said to myself, In there.

Myself said nothing.

The dig:

—Stanley, Looking for "Himself," Remembers the Dig—

Last May, one week after classes ended, I went on a dig with Dr. Madera and Golnaz to the Cahokia Mounds State Historic Site in Collinsville, Illinois. We carpooled in Dr. Madera's hatchback, which, though clean and uncluttered, smelled slept-in.

"It's 'Elena,'" said Dr. Madera, bopping the steering wheel. "We're in the field! Not the classroom."

Golnaz leaned from the passenger seat to give me a not-surprised look.

I returned it from the backseat, where I sat, excited, rolling a cigarette. My best professor. My smartest classmate. A light in a corridor—

—in Jail—

—a light ripped on at the end of the corridor.
   I looked away: I was sitting.
   Dr. Madera driving.
   Golnaz turning.
   The long broad landscapes of Illinois.
   The big good feeling I was feeling.
   The feeling of what was in front of me.
   The work—

—"Himself"—

—the big good work of excavation, physically and intellectu-
ally nutritious; the discovery of near-annihilated artifacts, fragments meaningless to most Americans, invaluable to us; many
days of intensive on-site labor, many weeks of intensive off-site
analyses; and, months later, the cautious conclusions that we'd
argue into existence, that would respond to the research conducted by our field's top scholars, that might in some small but
specific way advance what was known. I licked the seal on the
cigarette and passed it to Dr. Madera. She lowered her window
and lit up. I rolled one for myself. We zipped south on 55,
through fields of mega-farms, flattened squares of land and sky
and light. Dr. Madera, who spoke with throwaway confidence,
sounded even more right about everything, and Golnaz, who
asked sincere and careful questions, sounded even more insightful. We discussed recent unpleasant events in Chicago, where
we lived, and in Juárez, where Dr. Madera was born, and in
Tehran, where Golnaz was born. We agreed that things were
worse. We discussed relationships: how Dr. Madera's inept ex-
husband concocted excuses to call her, how Golnaz's depressed
brother-in-law had moved in with her and her husband and
son, and how T and I were living together, cohabitation with
a significant other a first for us both.

 Although we brought up our lives outside of class, and

didn't shy away from follow-up questions, our conversation only skipped across the surface of the personal—all of our anecdotes, however private they appeared, were appropriate for sharing with a stranger. From this shimmered a bright illusion of intimacy. We felt close, but weren't.

Dr. Madera and Golnaz wanted to know more about T.

"She's an actor," I said.

"Does she sing and dance also?" said Golnaz, while Dr. Madera said, "What's she in right now?"

I told them about *Black and White and Dead All Over*, the play that had been accepted to the festival in Prague.

"That's got to be noir," said Dr. Madera.

—Shadows in the Corridor—

Shadows split the light.
    Men or women walking.
    Shadows tripped, shadows dragged.
    I put my hands over my face:

We passed a semi loaded up with half a house. I explained the play, which Afiya had written: it followed the actors, writers, and producers of an imaginary old-time radio drama, also called *Black and White and Dead All Over*, and took place during the show's last episode. It was about deception, love, and identity, especially racial identity. The actors wore black and white costuming, and the lighting and makeup created a high contrast, making all white whiter and all black blacker. Overall, the play couldn't be called "realistic," but its departures from reality were surprising and entertaining, even moving. T played a big role: the lead actor in the radio drama, a "real life" ingénue "playing" a femme fatale.

Golnaz found it on her phone and bought tickets for her family.

Despite film noir's origin in France, said Dr. Madera, the genre had always seemed quintessentially American to her. Its fixation on the conflict between written and unwritten law. The equal-measure adoration of the lawman and the outlaw. Latino noir was terrific too, she added, though different in what it revealed about Latino cultures.

Golnaz said that we were detectives.

"Boring ones who follow boring laws," said Dr. Madera.

I asked Golnaz if there was any Iranian noir.

"Most definitely," she said, and began to explain, but Dr. Madera stomped the brakes—our seat belts lashed—we swerved and hit something, the something ka-thunked and clattered—we slid, we straightened, we slowed. The car wobbled. We crossed the rumble strip and stopped on the shoulder.

"That was a duffel bag," said Dr. Madera.

She got out of the car and I followed. A warm wind rolled, turning over into farmland. The front driver's-side tire hissed. We walked to the wayback and hauled out the bags, our luggage and groceries and equipment, which we piled on the shoulder. Golnaz offered to help—we waved her off. We opened the well, popped out the jack, and unscrewed the doughnut. Dr. Madera changed the tire and I assisted, handing her tools and holding things, while cars and trucks ripped by, rocking the hatchback, sending sound waves thudding through our bodies. We speculated on the contents of the duffel bag. I guessed bricks, she guessed briefcases full of cash. She wiped her hands on her shorts, smudging her thighs black. She was in her late thirties, a sturdy woman with a knockout smile, the most comfortable-with-every-situation person I knew.

A state trooper pulled over, lights on.

Dr. Madera smiled. She tightened the last two lug nuts, jumped to her feet, and went to meet the trooper. I put the jack and the flat in the well. When I turned around, the two of them were walking over.

"Who's she?" said the trooper, meaning Golnaz.

"Also my student," said Dr. Madera.

The trooper looked at our pile of bags. Then she looked at Dr. Madera. "License and registration," she said.

Dr. Madera went to fetch her documents.

The trooper asked me where we were coming from and where we were headed. I told her. A second trooper pulled up behind the first. Dr. Madera returned with the information, which the trooper took back to her cruiser. We waited, leaning on the open hatch, saying nothing. A mail truck howled by, two trailers long. The trooper came back and asked if we wouldn't mind opening a few bags. "Porque no?" said Dr. Madera. She unzipped them one by one. While the trooper used a metal wand to poke through our belongings, Dr. Madera caught her up on the Cahokians—how they were this continent's great forgotten ancient indigenous civilization, how they'd created a city more advanced, populous, and culturally rich than London was at the time.

"Their society collapsed," said Dr. Madera. "They couldn't get along with their neighbors."

"Lot of drug runners coming through here," said the trooper. "You have a nice day."

We returned to the road.

"Wow, I am very glad that she did not find my secret marijuana drugs," said Golnaz.

I told a high school story about getting pulled over after picking up Torrentelli and Barton from a St. Patrick's Day party. I'd borrowed my dad's car without asking, driven the forty minutes from Joliet to LaGrange, and collected the two of them from Barton's shithead cousin's house—I was sober, they were sloppy—and as soon as we turned the corner at the end of the block, a cruiser zoomed up behind us. The cop shouted us out of the car. He searched the front and the back and the trunk, throwing things around, flinging open all four doors, swearing that he'd find our alcohol, until his radio firecrackered with code speech—he stopped—he bolted back to his cruiser—he sped away, lights on, sirens off, leaving us standing there, staring at the ransacked car, Barton with a pint of whiskey in his jacket and Torrentelli with a half-smoked joint behind his ear.

Dr. Madera said that that was a white person's story, all right. She told one about her first dig as an undergrad at the University of New Mexico, a trip to Puzzle House in Colorado.

At the border between the states a Colorado trooper pulled her over, for speeding, and made her and her four classmates vacate the car while he searched it. One of Dr. Madera's best friends had stuffed a handle of tequila into his backpack, which he'd left on the seat. The neck-and-cap poked out between the zippers. It hadn't been opened, but the officer took everyone's licenses anyway. "New Mexico IDs are easy to fake," he said. He ran them in his car. When he gave them back, he pronounced everyone's names perfectly—they were all Mexican American—the officer didn't seem to be—and right before he left, he said, "Don't forget: you're in America, now."

"Which, for the region, I wouldn't call 'racist,'" said Dr. Madera.

We exited for Collinsville and found an auto parts store. Pickups lined the parking lot, tricked out or rust-pocked. We put on a new tire.

At the hotel, we agreed to meet in a few hours to figure out dinner.

For the first three nights we'd stay at the hotel. Then we'd settle in at the house on the outskirts of St. Louis that Dr. Madera had rented every summer since she'd joined the dig, the place she called Green Door. As a second-year MA graduate student, I'd heard nothing but sacred fondness for Green Door, even from the most ground-down dead-in-the-eyes fifth-year PhDs. Green Door was where they'd found deep refreshment after burning all day at the site. It was where they'd showered and changed and had the drink they felt they'd earned. It was where they'd cooked up big dinners, lazed on the porch to watch whole-sky sunsets, and stayed up later than they should have to argue about how the lives of ancient men and women had been lived, what those lives might have meant, back then, and what those lives could mean now, today. More than one person in the program had said, "Bury me at Green Door."

The only reason that we weren't already at Green Door,

Dr. Madera had reported, was because Miss Vera, the owner, was using it to put up relatives from out of state. They'd come to town for a birdwatching conference.

"Don't those people have birds where they're from?" said Dr. Madera.

I key-carded into my room, hopped into the middle of the bed, and turned the TV on right to a Sox game. Our bullpen was blowing a lead. It didn't matter. I rolled cigarette after cigarette, stocking my old-fashioned "smoking case," a gift from Ro that I'd rediscovered while packing for the trip. I didn't like to think about Ro. We'd both wanted it to work. But thinking about her there, in a hotel in Collinsville on the day before my first dig, I felt hopeful, hopeful that she was one day away from doing a thing she'd always wanted to do, a thing she might've never done if we'd stayed together. I rolled the twentieth cigarette, placed it in the case, and shut the lid. Then I rolled a twenty-first and strolled outside to smoke it. Maybe she was boarding that plane to Bangalore. Work vans and six-wheeled pickups chugged down the strip, rumbling. I walked to a gas station across the way to buy pop and snacks. The grandma behind the counter greeted me with a manly head-nod. Next to the register, where my neighborhood gas station showcased bowls of bananas, sat a grease-smudged jar of "GENUINE 'HOME MADE' DOUGH-NUTS." I asked for three. Behind the counter was a shelf of booze. At its far end stood a dusty fifth of off-brand tequila.

"*That's* racist," said Dr. Madera, when I gave it to her in the lobby.

Golnaz, smiling, set off for cups and ice.

Dr. Madera examined the bottle in a loving way. "I don't really like tequila," she said.

We sat with our drinks in big generic chairs by the entrance. Dr. Madera ordered pizza from a local joint, enough to offer leftovers to the other half of the field team, who'd be stopping by, she said. They'd been on the dig for a week already—

they'd rented a house outside St. Louis, too. "But their house is definitely a shithole," said Dr. Madera. The lobby doors opened: a dozen elderly white couples walked and walkered and wheel-chaired over to check-in, fresh off a tour bus. They brought a slow chatter and a clean smell. One joyous old woman shouted, "Exotic St. Louis!" A sweaty man arrived with our pizzas. They gleamed with pooled grease, the crust thin and crisp. We dug in. I passed out doughnuts for dessert. Golnaz refilled our cups. Dr. Madera gave us each the same gift—*Sacred Centers*. She reminisced about being a grad student. "All those hours with the data, compiling, charting, graphing!" she said, as we flipped through the pages. "But I loved it. I still do. I didn't know there'd be such poetry in it."

Golnaz wondered out loud about the use of the word *po-etry* to describe things that weren't poetry, how the compari-son elevated or satirized. She shifted in her chair, folding her legs up under her. She had five years on me, at least, but looked five years younger, a petite but solid person. Her precise way of speaking brought to mind an expert witness at the stand—calm and careful.

"The poetry in work," she said. "The poetry in choosing one's profession."

"The poetry in hand-rolled cigarettes," said Dr. Madera, miming one at me.

Outside I lit her up.

She pronounced me a bad influence.

I told her that T and I had made a pact to quit by June 1. "We want a smoke-free summer. We want to feel good."

Saying this out loud embarrassed me.

Dr. Madera kept her cigarette an arm's length away, so that the cherry's running smoke didn't trail onto her. She exhaled hard from the side of her mouth.

"Nowadays I only smoke OPs," she said.

I hadn't heard of those.

"Other people's."

I was supposed to laugh, and did.

"What the poets do," she said, "makes what we do valuable." Her favorites were Neruda and Paz and Sexton, and more recently, Natalie Diaz and Karla Kelsey. She talked about poetry as the mother discipline of every social science, as the original experiment-based investigation into every observable realm of human experience, just as subject to logically progressive principles of truth. We smoked another cigarette. I was relieved that she had so much to say, that she didn't require anything of me except to listen. I didn't want to talk about how happy I was feeling. Anything I could say, if said the way I'd want to say it, wouldn't sound true.

Golnaz had fallen asleep in her chair. Somehow she looked tense—she glowered in a dream, her body bunched up. When we sat down, she stirred. She brightened. "Bedtime," she said, sounding all the way awake.

Dr. Madera wondered where the other half of the field team was.

I suggested that we do another drink.

"No thanks," said Dr. Madera, checking her phone. "Maybe they got a flat."

We took the elevator to our floor together and said good night. Our rooms were close, but didn't share walls.

In bed I called T. She'd gone to Milwaukee for the weekend to hang out with Afiya. If she stayed alone in an apartment for too long, she said, she succumbed to feelings of cinematic desperation.

Her voice bobbed up from a noisy bar.

"Wait," she sang.

She hustled outside, the crowd sucking away.

I waited with a grin. Her voice was big without being showy, sure without being smug. It had body, texture, movement, range. If I missed what she said, it was because I leaned too close to how she said it.

"We're at Wolski's," she said.

"It's Polish—like you!" she said.

She described Wolski's real metal darts and real cork dart-boards and how you could play for free and eat free popcorn, and if you stayed until they closed at 2 a.m., they gave you a bumper sticker that read I CLOSED WOLSKI'S.

A dude on the street asked her for a cigarette.

"Are you old enough to vote?" she said to him.

"But did you vote?" she said to him.

"Milwaukee is druuuuuunk tonight," she said to me.

"Milwaukee better call a cab," she said.

"Milwaukee better get some food in its belly," she said.

"I can't believe I just worried about Milwaukee getting some food in its belly," she said.

"Oh!" she said, and she cupped her mouth, making her voice less distinct, and louder: she whispered that Afiya's boy-friend, an outdoorsy Wisconsin-proud man's man named Dunn, was finally going to propose to her.

"He asked for my help with the ring!" she said. "Just now! When Afiya went to get more popcorn!"

I rose from the hotel bed, alarmed.

One month ago I'd asked Afiya for *her* help in picking out a ring for T. I'd called her and she'd answered in what sounded like a crowded coffee shop.

"I'm supposed to be excited that you're doing this, Stan," Afiya had said. "And I am. But I want you to think about it. I want you to be sure."

"I'm sure and I've thought about it," I said.

Afiya told me about her kid brother and the woman he'd married, a story I'd heard from T: an angry ultimatum, an angry wedding, three angry infidelities, and a slow, sad, life-devouring divorce.

"They weren't sure," she said.

"Yes."

"They didn't think about it."

"Yes."

Someone asked a question that made Afiya chuckle. She called the question-asker one impatient motherfucker. An espresso machine clanked and rattled: she was behind the counter, making a drink.

To me she said, "T is my best friend. T is my girl."

"T is my best friend also, that's why I want to marry her."

"How do you know she'll say yes?"

I said that if she wasn't going to help, that was fine, just say so. I hung up.

She called me back.

"I shouldn't respect you for being so crazy-sensitive," she said. "But I do. I'm a romantic."

With suggestions from Afiya I settled on a style, something classic and simple. I ordered, I paid with my card, I waited. I took the L downtown to the jeweler, a bored and distant man who wore no jewelry himself, not even a ring, and I took the L back to our apartment, where I sat at the table and opened the box and put the ring in my palm. T had just left for rehearsal—the apartment smelled like her body wash. I searched myself for feelings of commitment, and then for feelings of relief.

I decided not to think about what I hadn't found until after the dig.

Outside Wolski's, T said, "It's what Afiya wants! But she has trouble saying yes to what she wants."

I paced the hotel room. Afiya had promised to keep our conversation a secret, but she might have made a different promise to T, and told her, in which case T telling me about Dunn might have been her way of letting me know that she knew I'd bought a ring. The idea of T knowing knocked cracks through me. I wanted to confess: I wanted to tell T that I'd be proposing to her despite the fact that I wasn't sure, that what I *was* sure about was that being in a relationship with her was better than being in a relationship with anyone I'd ever known because of how she enabled me to forget myself, which was maybe just a way of saying that when I was with her, I was happy with who I wasn't.

She'd be who she was and who I was would drop.

A different dude on the street asked T for a cigarette. He wanted to know if anyone had ever told her that she looked exactly like a local anchorwoman.

"It's news to me," she said to him.

She asked about my day.

I told her I was happy and excited but nervous.

She said she had a feeling that first thing tomorrow I'd discover a legendary artifact with magical properties. An international adventure would ensue. It'd be dangerous, but I'd save America. And Poland. And afterwards, Hollywood and the Polish equivalent of Hollywood would team up to make a movie about me.

"Kiełbasawood," she said. "Do they call it Kiełbasawood?"

"You don't want me making movies for Kiełbasawood," she said.

Afiya shouted at T for a cigarette.

"Is that still Stan?" shouted Afiya.

"How do you get Stan to talk that much?" shouted Afiya.

"It's weird not being around you," T said to me. "I think about you a lot when you're not around, probably more than I do when you're around. This thing happens where the you in my head isn't really the actual you. You know? Stanley-in-My-Head is pretty cool and thoughtful and hairy and handsome, he's maybe even *more* of all those things, and then I start to feel bad about that, like I'm holding you up to impossible imaginary standards. But then I talk to Actual You or see Actual You. And wow, you're so much better than the supposedly better you in my head."

I said I liked Actual T best too. Though Imaginary T had a lot going for her also.

We said, "I love you."

"Wait," I said, before she hung up.

I could hear her smiling.

I said, "I'm going to propose to you."

She said nothing. Then she said, "I didn't hear that?"

"I'm going to propose to you."

"Ah!" she said.

"I'm—that's—ah!" she said.

I felt her put up her truth-face.

"You sound like you're talking yourself into it," she said.

I started to say something that wasn't true.

"No," she said. "You're saying it out loud because you want me to hold you accountable, you want me to help you talk yourself into it."

She revisited our most recent marriage talk, from a month ago, when she'd explained why being married was important to her, when I'd explained why being married wasn't important to me, when we'd explained ourselves into silence.

"It's a big important thing you're saying," she said. "I'm worried you don't mean it how you're supposed to."

I said something that was half-true.

"Stanley. You know I want to go there with you, to wedding-land. I'm not a mysterious person. But I'm only going to go to wedding-land with someone who wants to go there with me. I'm not going to talk you into it, is what I'm saying. You know this: I tried that in my last relationship. I can't do it again. I don't want to. No."

I started to say something else that wasn't true, but stopped. Then I said, "You thought you could change Ibrahim's mind about what marriage is, what marriage could be, so you tried to. You don't think you can change mine."

"That's true. Yes. But it's also true that I was a different person then, in a different relationship. And if you're suggesting that it's somehow my responsibility to 'think that I can change your mind,' please get the fuck off the phone and put the other Stanley on, the Stanley who makes sense."

"I'm working on becoming a different person," I said.

"How else do you do that but by talking yourself into taking uncomfortable actions, by being talked into taking uncomfortable actions."

"But you don't want to be a different person."

I said I did.

"*I* don't want you to be a different person," she said.

"A different person is what we need."

There was a pause; in it was a giving up.

"This might be as far as we can go," said T.

—Stanley with Himself—

Footsteps scuffled and slapped.

—the Dig—

"I should head back in," said T. "I need to be happy for Afiya."

I tried to think of something to say to that.

"Bye," she said.

I lay back in bed, shut my eyes, and set my hands on my chest. I felt like I'd shoved myself into a sack. T was right: I wanted to be talked into it; T was wrong: I wanted to be a different person, a person who could go further than where we were. I went over what I'd said, trying to unhitch what I meant from what I didn't. My mouth puckered, tequila-dry, but I didn't get up for a glass of water.

When I woke to my alarm at five, I saw texts from T, sent late:

> don't you think that if you do something big and
>   important like propose it's because on some
>   level you were going to do it anyway, not
>   because you were talked into it?
> but maybe that's just me being hopeful
> people really want these bumper stickers, i got you
>   one
> also they gave us panties, wolskis panties, wtf!
> dude on the street is dick out and walking

> backwards and pissing, his friends are telling
> him not to cheat
> getting two cheeseburger pizzas
> did you buy a ring

I wrote: "I did." Then I deleted that and wrote, "I'm going to propose to you as soon as I get back," and I deleted that and wrote, "I was going to propose to you as soon as I got back," and I deleted that and wrote, "I wanted to," and I deleted that. I decided that "I did" was enough. I sent it.

I filled a glass of water at the sink. It tasted soapy.

Then I saw that I'd sent all five messages:

I did
I'm going to propose to you as soon as I get back
I was going to propose to you as soon as I got back
I wanted to
I did

—an Artist—

I removed my hands from my face.

The footsteps and the shadows and the light condensed into two men.

One of the men, a police officer, was speaking to me.

He was walking away.

A heavy man stepped up. He held an envelope, the one that was labeled EVIDENCE: COMPLETE EXPLANATION OF THE MADE-UP MAN. It still had a sketch of my face on the front. It was still sealed shut.

The heavy man said, "My name is Information."

I turned around on the cot to face the wall. I closed my eyes.

The man became his voice: his voice was emotional.

"I am working for Lech," he said, "but I am also working for you. I will offer you information, and I will offer information to Lech. I am on no one's side. I am my own side."

There was the sound of the unsealing and opening of the envelope.

Then the sound of a sheet of paper being pulled out.

"This case is 'The Case of the Made-Up Man.'"

The sound of another sheet.

"The mystery is: 'Am I actual?'"

Another sheet.

"The crime is: 'What has Lech done? What is Lech doing

now? What is Lech going to do next?' And: 'What has Stanley done?'"

Another sheet.

"Stanley is the detective; or is Stanley the client?"

The heavy man sighed.

"Manny is the detective's sidekick; or is Manny the villain's sidekick? Abbey is the femme fatale; or is Abbey the ingénue? T is the ingénue; or is T the femme fatale, or the detective's sidekick, or the villain's sidekick, or the villain, or the separate detective investigating a separate mystery, crime, and case? Lech is the villain and Lech is the client. I am Information."

The heavy man was crying.

"There are other characters, playing other roles," he said. "They are very important. They are Stanley's family and friends. But I know nothing about them. I do not know why I know nothing about them. It is who I am to know. This morning, I ate breakfast. I gathered information—I looked and listened, I smelled, I tasted and touched. I thought and remembered. I ate lunch. I traded the information that I gathered for more information, and I used that information to gather even more information. I ate dinner. Here is the challenge: I did not associate myself with the information. Do you understand? This is an impossible task, to not associate. I only counted the information—I categorized it and I stored it. I went to bed. Do I have a family? Do I have a friend? It is no way to live, it is not a life. It is as if I am an artist."

Another sheet.

"As the detective, Stanley follows a code. Here is Stanley's code: 'Say no.'"

Another sheet.

"As the sidekick to the detective or the villain, Manny follows the detective."

Another sheet.

"As the femme fatale, Abbey has an angle. Here is her angle: 'I want to help Stanley but I want to help myself.'"

Another sheet.

"As the ingénue, T has a story. Here is her story: 'I want to help Stanley but I want to help myself but I don't want to help myself if what it costs is helping Stanley but I don't want to help Stanley if what it costs is helping myself.'"

Another sheet.

"As the villain and client, Lech has a motive. Here is his motive: 'I want to give Stanley the help that he does not want, and is not able to ask for, but needs.' And: 'I want to give Abbey back to her art.' And: 'I want to give myself a project in which the participants, as in life, are not asked for permission—in which their agency, as in life, is the least essential part of their identity.'"

Another sheet.

"The setting is the self."

Another sheet.

"The location is Stanley."

Another sheet.

"The plot is: 'The Opening of the Case, the Investigation, the Betrayals, the Damage, the Truths, the Closing of the Case.'"

Another sheet.

"The writers are Lech and Abbey. The producer is Lech. The consultants are Lech, Abbey, Janet, Dennis, Thomas, T, and Manny. The editor is Lech. The director is Stanley."

There was the sound of placing sheets back into an envelope.

The heavy man was crying hard.

"What information do you have for me?" he said.

"Take your time," he said.

"Think," he said.

I was thinking.

"Is there anything?" he said.

I covered my ears.

—the Dig—the Site of the Dig—

I texted T to say that I hadn't meant to send her what I'd sent her, that I'd call her on a break to explain it. I showered and shaved. I went downstairs to the self-service hotel cafeteria, where Golnaz, alone, frowned at a hissing waffle iron. She opened the hatch to a waffle with ideal golden-brownness.

When she saw me, her frown fell; her usual serene look sprang back.

"Ready?" she said.

I might've nodded. I stuffed a bagel into the toaster. It was slow, so I poured a cup of coffee and sat with Golnaz.

"I dreamed that it would rain dried-out dead bodies," she said. She nudged the weather page of the *St. Louis Post-Dispatch* toward me. "It won't. It will be nice out."

When I scooted up to read the forecast I dropped my coffee. The cup hit my feet—coffee drenched my workboots, soaked my socks.

Golnaz handed me napkins.

Dr. Madera walked in. She looked at us blotting at the spill. "They're here," she said.

We stood up.

"Did you eat?" she said.

We said we had.

We met the rest of the team in the lobby. Dr. Bauer, the

project director, a professor from a university with a more famous program than ours, introduced himself as Curt. He was tall enough to play college basketball, but hunched, with a squinty, sunburned, bothered face. He wore a faded fedora with two white feathers in it.

Dr. Madera gave him a hug. This annoyed him, which pleased her.

Throughout the semester, Dr. Madera had told comic anecdotes about Curt, whom she'd known since grad school, whom she called "Mr. Prickly."

"Ask Mr. Prickly how he earned his hat feathers," she'd said to Golnaz and me on the drive down.

He didn't seem like the sort of man who wanted to be asked about his hat feathers.

Golnaz and I shook Curt's hand, and then the hands of Haley, Rishi, and Mieszko, our student counterparts. No mention was made of how they hadn't swung by for leftover pizza last night. We lined up on separate sides of our professors, like we were about to play a pick-up game of stickball. Curt briefed us on the progress they'd made in the week they'd been there (the removal of most of the sterile backfill, the updating of databases) and the plan for what we'd get done that day (the completion of the removal of the backfill). The excavation itself—the digging, the sifting, the brown-bagging—would start today, he said, but only as a precaution (to ensure that the last centimeters of backfill hadn't blended with the first centimeters of the site) and as practice (for the rookies). The "real" excavation, so to speak, would begin tomorrow. Everyone listened to Curt and looked ready. I listened, but I didn't know how I looked; how I was feeling about last night's talk with T had seeped into how I was feeling about the dig. I was dull with fear, and at the same time, jumpy.

We drove to the Cahokia Mounds State Historic Site. Mounds rose up on both sides of Collinsville Road, looking like naturally occurring hills, not like the man-made monuments they were, planned structures built by the citizens of a sophisticated civilization. Some were shaggy with coarse grasses, some were mowed close. All were treeless and dewy-bright. We passed Woodhenge, the reconstructed circle of ceremonial sun-tracking posts, and then a pair of mounds I recognized from research but couldn't place, and then Monks Mound, the biggest earthwork in the Americas, a hulking multi-platformed mass, high in these flatlands, taller and wider and slumpier than I'd imagined. My window went opaque with sun. I rolled it all the way down. At my surprise birthday party, Barton had said that when he was a boy his dad had taken him to mounds in Ohio, an educational detour on the way to his grandpa's. He'd found them underwhelming, memorable only for how forgettable they were. I raised my phone and took a picture from the window. Now that I was seeing them for the first time, I understood how, for most Americans, "ancient monument" meant "stone"—pillared temples and pyramids—and consequently, these constructions, made of earth, not only "couldn't" represent a socially complex long-gone culture, but reinforced the false belief brought to the Americas by European settlers that indigenous mound-building societies weren't advanced enough to attempt, achieve, or deserve permanence, much less a place on the high school curriculum.

Outside of Barton and my classmates, no one I'd mentioned the mounds to had heard of them.

We turned at the sign for the Interpretive Center, marked with the image of the Birdman Tablet, and parked. Inside we met a member of the site staff, a thorough man who gave us maps and informed us about the other excavations, the teams from the University of Michigan, Washington University, and the University of Bologna, in Italy. Then we drove across the highway, through the parking lot for Monks Mound, and onto a field. We bumped over grass and up to Trego Mound.

Our job would be to resume the excavation that Curt had

first proposed fourteen years ago, that had been opened and ongoing for nine, that Dr. Madera had partnered with him on for the last eight. In the 1920s, D. Maximilian Doty, an unscrupulous logging baron turned amateur archaeologist, had dug a series of step trenches into Trego Mound. His workers discovered human remains, a necklace fragment, whelk shell shards, and artisans' tools. Of what was found, only the artisans' tools had landed in the Cahokia Mounds State Historic Site's collection; Curt had examined them for his doctoral dissertation. He argued that their existence indicated the presence of a nearby toolmaking workshop, one that might even have been on Trego Mound. But he was more interested in the soil-sample records that D. Maximilian Doty had compiled, which suggested that Trego Mound was in fact a "mound-within-mounds": a pair of conical mounds that had been "buried" into a single platform mound. The dig's objectives, then, were to (a) relocate the limits of the 1920s excavation, (b) expand on the 1920s excavation, (c) study the mound's composite construction, and (d) determine if future excavations should be conducted to search for a toolmaking workshop.

"We're searching for reasons to do more searching," Dr. Madera had said. "Which is a pretty good definition of 'contemporary archaeology.'"

Last semester, Golnaz and I had co-written a paper on Trego Mound, the mounds that were part of its grouping, and the 1920s excavation. I'd focused my share of the research on one unknown: in addition to the tools, the workers had uncovered the bones of a man who'd been buried without his head. In its place were what turned out to be the remains of a ceramic pot.

—What Is Known About the Man Who'd Been Buried Without His Head—

The remains of the headless man and the pot had been sold at least four times in the 1920s and '30s, from D. Maximilian Doty to a reputable private collector to a semi-reputable short-lived museum to a disreputable eugenicists' association to an unknown and almost certainly disreputable private collector. Then they were lost.

—What Is Not—

I wondered what was put in the pot.

I wondered where the head was put.

I wondered what ritual the burial had been put inside of (the ritual that enriched the burial with meaning), and what myth this ritual had been put inside of (the myth that sustained the ritual's meaning), and what the people who participated in the burial (the high-status citizens who served as functionaries and the low-status citizens who served as witnesses) had done to the myth to make it fit into their lives, or conversely, what they had done to their lives to make them fit into the myth.

Then I wondered why I didn't mind not knowing the answers to these questions.

Because that's what you love about anthropology, T had said.

I asked her what that was.

The same thing I love about acting: guessing at how to be good at being somebody else.

—Dig—

Dr. Madera put the car in park. We grabbed our gear.

Trego Mound was a low flattened hump, no different in appearance from most of its neighbor mounds. Several summer volunteers were already up top. They stood at the shade-tented picnic table, sharing a bottle of sunscreen. Curt introduced them, emphasizing how far they'd come to work here: Charlie, a retired advertising executive from San Francisco, Mary-Beth and Nirupama, two Australian Army engineers from Melbourne, and Wu, a sculptor from Shanghai.

"The mounds are magnets," said Dr. Madera.

The tarps that covered the site in the off-season had been peeled back, weighted with cinder blocks and dump piles. They crinkled underfoot. I stepped to the edge of the exposed excavation trench. I'd seen hundreds of pictures of trenches, and dozens of pictures of this trench—I recognized the dimensions, the size of the darkness, the right-angled exactness—but in person, it had the feel of a work of public art. I thought of my aunt. I touched the dirty ladder that led to the bottom. Even Curt could stand down there and disappear.

Dr. Madera paired me with Haley, an upbeat undergrad, square and strong with youth. Most of her face was her smile. She'd worked on-site last summer.

Golnaz, Rishi, and Mieszko unpacked equipment.

"Get digging," said Curt.

Haley laughed. "He can't not say that."

We clattered down the ladder, out of the early sun, and into a pocket of night. The air was cold and damp, the walls were soft and musty. Black moths bounced off my face. Everything I'd learned about this mound from D. Maximilian Doty's notes, experts' commentary on those notes, and Curt's scholarly articles sank away—the smell of the trench was the smell of being a kid. I remembered wrestling with my brother on a berm by the highway; I remembered finding clay pits at the Indiana Dunes with Torrentelli and Barton, scooping out handfuls, smearing our faces, starting a clayball fight; I remembered sundown games of capture the flag, stalking through neighbors' backyards, hoping that if I crossed paths with someone, I'd see them before they saw me.

I remembered hiding from Busia behind a heap of mulch.

"Shit damn hell!" she'd screamed.

"Got it?" said Haley.

I said I got it. She'd been explaining their system.

"It's just keeping it even," she said. "One zone at a time. It'll go fast!"

We shoveled backfill into wheelbarrows.

The Australians pushed the wheelbarrows to the dump pile.

We shoveled.

They pushed.

It was the kind of work I knew, which should have settled me, but didn't. I felt like I did when I overdressed.

More than once, Dr. Madera had said, "So much of archaeology has so little to do with archaeology."

Haley and I bent at the same time and bumped butts. I dropped my shovel.

"We're dancing!" she said, waggling her hips.

Sunlight rectangled into the trench.

The shade had a springlike chill, the light a summery heat.

Curt appeared at the edge, holding a clipboard.

"Good," he said.

I turned too quickly and nearly hacked Haley's face with my shovel.

"Whoa!" she said, sidestepping.

"You picked a proper place for a murder, anyway," said one of the Australians.

"The burial's half-done!" said the other.

Curt observed.

We worked in the shade. We worked in the sun.

The smell of the soil shifted.

"Curt?" said Haley.

We climbed out, Curt climbed in. He crouched. He picked at the soil and rubbed it between his fingers. From above, his hat looked like it belonged on the head of a hobo-clown.

"Trowels," he said, standing. "Sift what's left."

The Australians set up the sifters.

At the picnic table, the retired advertising executive and the sculptor coded the last of the brown bags.

"You two," said Curt, climbing out.

Haley had brought her own trowel, a shiny model in a pouch. I pulled a crusty one from a communal tool bag. We went into the trench, we went onto our knees. A stale coffee-stink punched up from my socks. My stomach popped and growled.

Curt watched. "Go slow," he said.

I went too slow.

"No," said Curt. "Haley, show him."

"Like this," she said.

I went too fast.

"No," said Curt.

I went too hard and I went too light.

"Haley," said Curt.

"It's tricky at first," said Haley.

Curt said, "Up here."

I left the trench; Mieszko took my place. The Australians sifted. The retired advertising executive and the sculptor had disappeared. Golnaz clicked at a laptop at the picnic table. Dr. Madera and Rishi stood at a total station, surveying.

"iPad," said Curt.

I found his iPad and brought it over and when I handed it to him I dropped it.

"No," said Curt, stopping me, picking it up himself.

I went to the cooler for a bottle of water. I drank it as slowly as I could.

At noon, the retired advertising executive and the sculptor showed up with trays of meat and sides from a St. Louis barbecue.

Curt said, "Eating-time."

We walked off-mound to a circle of skinny trees, where we unfolded blankets and sat in shade. From there we had a side view of Monks Mound: the curving paved path to its foot, the steep stairs to its wide platform top. It was a state park. Locals and tourists strolled and jogged, on their own and with babies. A man in military fatigues marched up the stairs, down the stairs, up the stairs, a sandbag tucked into his backpack. Dr. Madera undid the covers on the food and Rishi and Mieszko distributed napkins and plates. I stared at Monks Mound, working to remember why I was there. Thousands of years ago, men and women had settled this land to hunt, fish, and farm. For a while it went well. Their village teemed into a town, their town into a city, their city into a cultural capital, their cultural capital into a powerful continental trade center. They built mounds. From the mounds their leaders ran ceremonies, sacrifices, feasts. Sometimes they lived on the mounds, sometimes they buried their dead in them. Time and weather buried what they didn't. What we dug up could teach us about these people, but we'd never know the basics, including the names they'd given to this place and to themselves—"Cahokia" and "Cahoki-ans" were terms derived from the name of a tribe that happened to be in the area when blundering Trappist monks arrived in the seventeenth century, a few hundred years after the city's abandonment. Most of what could be known could no longer be known.

—Ears Covered, Eyes Closed—an Artist—

The smell of perfume, the smell of cologne.

Herbs and flowers. Spices and smoke.

I opened my eyes and I dropped my hands from my ears: I was facing the wall.

A person was walking the corridor, passing my cell.

What he or she was wearing was rustling and jingling, ticking and scraping, snapping.

A costume, an outfit, a uniform.

I wasn't looking.

He or she was passing me.

Fruits and soils—earth, juice, wind.

He or she passed me.

He or she reached the end of the corridor and stopped.

I didn't look.

I said to myself: You can't see.

Then he or she sang. The singing was skilled.

I was hearing the singing—I was hearing the song.

As I was hearing the song I was forgetting it. I was forgetting its rhythm and melody, I was forgetting if it had words or didn't, I was forgetting what all of its elements together were making me feel, think, imagine.

It was going in as a real something and coming out as a nothing.

—the End of the Dig—

I fixed up a brisket sandwich with too much brisket in it.

Curt and Dr. Madera debated other local lunch options.

The volunteers eased into an exchange of inside jokes.

Golnaz started a get-to-know-you conversation: Haley was from East St. Louis; Rishi from Sugar Land, Texas; Mieszko from Szczecin, a Polish city near the German border.

"Stanley is Polish," said Golnaz.

Mieszko nodded. He had a rumpled, sleepy look. "Many from Chicago are."

Rishi smiled at this. His smile was smarmy.

I went for seconds.

Haley said, "What do you think we'll find this summer?"

I fixed up a pulled pork sandwich with too much pulled pork in it.

"Post molds," said Golnaz.

"Whelk shells," said Mieszko.

"Whelk shells and post molds," said Rishi.

Haley said she hoped we'd find human bones, though she knew it wasn't likely that we would. "Last summer, at their site, the Italians found a zygomatic fragment," she said. "That would make my life!"

Dr. Madera and Curt remembered a professor they'd had, a sexist old man, ethically out of whack but well-respected by the professional community. Curt said that you could be a terrible person but a terrific scientist. Dr. Madera said no way. They bounced back and forth, their banter friendly, but not without a certain strain—they hurried to get to the more general points that they agreed on.

Rishi noticed that I noticed. He covertly mimed a penis going into a vagina, a gesture I hadn't seen since college.

I loped over for dessert.

"Stanley," said Golnaz. "What is your opinion?"

"We'll find a legendary artifact with magical properties. International adventure will ensue. We'll save America."

I'd meant it as a joke, but it came out caustic. I put two big brownies on my plate.

Rishi hadn't stopped staring at me. I stared back.

"You box, don't you," he said.

His nose, I noticed then, had been flattened more than once. He had a fighter's build: no-necked but long-armed, stocky-lanky. I told him that I'd boxed in high school and that in college I'd been in an early morning boxing workout group. I didn't tell him that for the last three weeks I'd been slugging the bag at the gym, doing footwork and strength-training, that I hoped it'd help me quit smoking next month.

"How could you tell?" said Golnaz to Rishi.

"You watch any MMA?" he said to me.

"My posture," I said to Golnaz.

He smiled again. "Not that."

I said I didn't watch MMA, not anymore.

"Why not?"

I'd sworn it off because I'd found myself eager to see fighters' faces destroyed. Without wanting to, I'd begun to root for heavyweight bouts to be determined by decision, no submissions, no knockouts, the men pounded round by round into lumbering wreckage, their faces bruised and bloodied, swollen and broken, simplified. After the winner was announced— when his arm was hoisted by a ref, when he howled and flexed and strutted—I'd be stricken with heavy shame. I felt complicit in their disfiguration.

"I stopped liking it," I said.

Rishi wanted to talk about an upcoming title fight, Roddewig versus "El Jeffecito."

I hadn't heard of them.

"Jeffecito throws a really weird hook to the body," he said, putting up his fists, demonstrating.

Part of what I'd appreciated about MMA was tracking how the fighters applied boxing techniques, how they modified them. But I didn't know what Rishi was talking about. I couldn't see it.

"Stand up," he said, standing up.

I did.

Rishi hopped around and threw a few practice jabs. Then he presented the punch stage by stage. I let his fist touch me. He explained why the form was unusual, something about the hip.

Everyone was watching.

"It's actually easier to see it faster," said Rishi.

"Go for it."

"Try to block it."

He hammered my side, fast, way too fast for me to block, and not even half as hard as he could. My organs joggled.

"You see that?"

"Yes," I said, but I hadn't.

He put up his guard. "Try it."

I'd met men like Rishi before, men who'd gone into martial arts to start fights with unskilled strangers at bars, who needed to knock big drunk wannabe brawlers onto their asses and into ambulances in order to arrive at end-of-the-night erections. It'd taken me until college to learn to walk away—first from being incited by them, then from becoming them.

But Curt said, "What the hell are you idiots doing."

And I said, "Try to block it," and Rishi said, "I will," and

I feinted with my left and swung with my right and cracked him in the ribs about as hard as he'd cracked me. My thumb popped.

He didn't show any sign of having been hit.

"Wow," he said, dropping his hands. "I'll be honest: I didn't think you had the balls to feint."

"Go fuck your mother," I said.

For a moment he was too surprised to be insulted.

Curt stepped up, looming.

"Pretend to be adults," he said. "Or go home."

"Hold up, we're cool," said Rishi, offering a handshake.

I sat instead.

The afternoon was used to remove and screen what was left of the backfill. Everyone ignored what had happened in their own way: Dr. Madera didn't seem to have noticed, Curt became oddly polite, Haley increased her chattiness, Rishi and Mieszko increased their silence, the volunteers avoided me, Golnaz exuded a competence, calm, and focus that gradually increased the competence, calm, and focus of everyone but me, and I tripped on a bucket.

"I do that once a day!" said Haley.

I worked at the sifters.

"Have you tried it like this?" said Curt.

I worked at a total station.

"Try that knob," said Curt.

"Almost," said Curt.

"The other way," said Curt.

I worked on the databases.

"This column," said Golnaz.

"This row," said Golnaz.

I sat on a far cinder block and smoked a cigarette. Dragonflies arced above me, pairing and unpairing. A hawk screamed. I flexed my thumb: it was swollen.

"Pack it in," said Curt. "Day's done."

We closed up the site.

On the ride to the hotel, Golnaz asked Dr. Madera a series of complicated technical questions about the database program. The interface was old, they agreed, and in some ways, needlessly complex. The only reason it was still used was that no one wanted to learn a new one.

"For my thesis I will design a new program," said Golnaz.

"So little of archaeology is archaeology," said Dr. Madera.

I stayed outside with a cigarette while they walked into the hotel.

"You shouldn't do that," said an old man in a wheelchair, on his way to the parking lot. He was rigged up with nose tubes and an oxygen tank.

"What my husband means is, he's envious," said his wife.

"Yes," he said.

I asked them how long they'd been married.

"Forty-nine years," said the woman.

"How do you like marriage."

"We don't," said the man.

"But that's what we like about it," said the woman.

"Yes," he said.

In my room I sat on the floor and called T. She didn't answer. I didn't leave a message. A squeaky panic screwed in on me, pulling tight. I imagined T and Afiya talking, smoking, drinking; I imagined T coming to a decision about us without me there. My brother had texted, wondering if we'd found a piece of the One True Cross and whether or not time-traveling Nazis had attempted to steal it yet, and my aunt had texted, asking if archaeologists were secret artists or if artists were secret archaeologists. I changed out of my clothes and I washed my face. My thumb hurt—it was hot. At the ice machine I filled a cup and jammed my hand in it.

The Sox were winning 12 to 1. The network replayed the first-inning grand slam, slow and tall to center field. A triumphant kid had caught it barehanded.

I took a break from icing to try to roll a cigarette and couldn't.

There was a knock at the door.

"Are you coming to dinner?" said Golnaz, when I let her in. She hadn't changed out of her field clothes. Around her hung the smell of sweat, sun, dirt.

"A challenging first day," she said, nodding. "It is normal."

I asked if it was challenging for her.

She looked at me strangely. "Yes, that is what I mean—it has been a challenging first day, for me."

I was sure that she was saying this to make me feel better.

We went to a Mexican restaurant cluttered with kitsch, with bright plastic parakeets and palm trees. Mariachi music bumped and trilled. Every surface, including the tables, smelled like mop water. The word *authentic* appeared in the description of every item on the menu. Dr. Madera ordered drinks and appetizers, in Spanish. Curt rolled his eyes. Two old white men, the only other party, sat at the next table, one of them donning an oversized FELIZ CUMPLEAÑOS sombrero. A server brought pitchers of margaritas and platters of taquitos and quesadillas. The margarita tasted like margarita-scented window cleaner. I drank it steadily. The problem wasn't that I was inherently bad at fieldwork, I said to myself, or that I was "distracted" into incompetence by what was happening with me and T. The problem was worse. The problem was that where there was supposed to be desire—where desire had once been, or where I'd mistakenly believed desire to have once been—was instead the incremental disintegration of that desire. I looked at Haley, who listened closely to Dr. Madera and Curt, waiting to put her word in; I felt sure that *desire* was a word for "talent." I looked at Golnaz, who listened closely to everyone, converting her observations into conversation-enhancing questions; I felt sure that *desire* was a word for "work ethic."

What I'd believed was my reason—the someone brighter,

the someone stranger, the someone I'd wanted to begin to become—was just some space at the center of myself that wasn't me.

Mieszko refilled my margarita, then his.

"Dziękuję," I said.

He nodded. "Dobje."

I shook my head, I motioned at the margarita: "Nie dobje."

He shrugged.

Curt said, "I'd like to hear what Stan thinks."

The conversation they'd been having came to an agreeable pause. Curt was being inclusive.

"I wasn't paying attention," I said.

Everyone but me ordered entrees.

Back at the hotel, Dr. Madera insisted on tequila.

We sat in the same chairs from the night before, only more loosely, more heavily. I didn't want to stay and drink, I didn't want to stand and go. Dr. Madera poured out doubles. She told the story of the first time she drank tequila, a complicated misadventure involving a family picnic, a one-legged cousin, a garbage-choked canal, and an encounter with a local talk-show host.

"I wish we were at Green Door," said Dr. Madera.

Golnaz, slightly drunk, said, "May I ask you a question?"

Dr. Madera laughed. "You may."

"It is a sensitive question."

"Please," said Dr. Madera, goofy-serious, "go on."

Golnaz sat up. She spoke carefully, fighting the slur that slanted her voice: "What I want to know is, what did you feel? On your first excavation. On the first day of your first excavation, afterwards. I am saying, was it what you expected? Was it not? What did you feel?"

Dr. Madera made a show of thinking about this. She uncapped the tequila. Golnaz finished what was in her cup, then held it out—Dr. Madera filled both their cups, then glanced at me.

I said I was good.

Dr. Madera leaned back. "What I felt after the first day of my first dig, above all, was disappointment."

She explained how the dig wasn't what she'd expected, experientially, even though it was exactly what she'd expected, procedurally.

"But it got better! I made it better. For myself."

Golnaz said, "If I may continue. What you are saying, it is very compelling. But. It is not very specific. What I want to know is, to make it better, to make it better for yourself, what do you adjust? Do you adjust your expectations of the work, or do you adjust your expectations of yourself?"

"You'd think there'd be a difference between one's expectations of the work and one's expectations of oneself. There isn't."

Golnaz started to ask another question, one with the trajectory of an objection, but her phone rang. She staggered off to answer it.

Dr. Madera and I stepped out for a smoke. We stood by the bushes and stared at the parking lot, at the roar and glow of 55. I waited for her to keep talking, but she didn't. She was as quiet as she'd been when we'd leaned on her hatchback and waited for the trooper to return with her papers. She might have been reviewing the day. She might have been trying to find a friendly way to tell me not to fuck up so much tomorrow.

"Sorry about today," I said, and at the same time, she said, "I used to have a truck like that."

Parked in front of us was a huge black pickup. All its windows tinted.

"Tinted windows, nice," I said, as she said, "What?"

"Sorry about what?" she said.

I couldn't tell if she truly didn't know what I was talking about, or if she was pretending not to know. Either option embarrassed me.

She raised an eyebrow, meaning, Spill it.

"For my fuckups in the field. For a day of fuckups."

"You call that fucking up? On a dig in Costa Rica, when I was a student, I was processing this ceramic figurine, it was a monkey. A constipated-looking monkey. I don't know how it happened, but when I was cleaning it, I knocked the fucking thing off the table. It almost looked like I did it on purpose. It hit the floor and broke in half—you can imagine how I felt. It was awful. The field director, he was standing next to me when it happened, he told me to stay right where I was—he rustled up whoever was around to come to the lab to look at me with my broken fucking monkey. Most of the team was there. He said, 'Because of her carelessness, Elena has just obliterated a link to the ancient world.' He kept going, he was working himself up, he said some shit about the journey of artifacts through time and our duty as stewards of that journey—shit that I believe in, by the way—and then he dismissed everybody except me. He called me a cunt. He picked up the two pieces of the monkey. He waved them around. He said, 'Well? What do you have to say for yourself, about what you've done to this artifact?' and he didn't want me to answer, he wanted me to just stand there and keep taking it."

Dr. Madera waited for me to ask her what she did.

I asked her what she did.

"I said to him, 'Now it's easier for you to shove it up your ass.'"

She mimed shoving two pieces of a monkey up an ass.

"Curt was on that dig," she said, smiling. "He didn't believe me when I told him what I said."

Golnaz puttered through the door, looking dazed, a hand-rolled cigarette in her mouth. I didn't remember giving her one, or ever seeing her smoke. She lit up. It was a joint.

She took long, slow hits.

"I don't miss my son and I don't miss my husband," she said.

She passed the joint to me. I did a short puff, offered it to Dr. Madera, who declined, and then I passed it back to Golnaz. Dr. Madera, trying not to laugh, gave me a look that said, Good for her!

"Why?" said Golnaz.

I turned my back to Dr. Madera and said to Golnaz that it wasn't that she didn't miss her family, it was that she loved what she was doing here. Being here was what she missed. Being here was what she'd been missing.

She brought the joint to her mouth but dropped it. It smoldered on the sidewalk. She stamped it out and said something in Farsi. She was crying.

"We have come to the end of what there is to be said about that," she said.

We walked her back through the lobby, into the elevator, down the hall, and to her room.

I gave her a hug.

"Thank you," she said.

She closed the door behind her gently, like she was worried she'd wake someone up.

Dr. Madera found all of this funnier than I did. "She'll figure it out," she said. "And if she doesn't, that's figuring it out, too. You wouldn't believe how many times I've seen this. You know what this is about?"

"Her family."

"Golnaz has it in her to be a great anthropologist."

I agreed.

"The world wants women to clip their wings. Even worse, it wants them to do it to themselves."

We walked to Dr. Madera's door. She cuffed me on the shoulder.

"I want you on board for Central America," she said.

The Central America trip, a four-week winter-break research intensive, was the trip that every grad student in our program wanted to be selected to take. The application process, which hadn't opened yet, was even more competitive than it was for Cahokia.

"You're good to have around," said Dr. Madera.

Then the way we looked at each other changed.

We didn't move.

The more we didn't move, the more the way we looked at each other changed. I could have looked away, I could have moved. I didn't. We were becoming two people who could kiss.

I kissed her.

She jumped back—her face twisted.

"No," she said, chopping the air with her hands, disgusted.

For an instant my sight punched out.

The world was a dumb white wall.

"Mira que cabrón," I heard her say.

"You have the wrong idea about me," she said.

My sight broke back—she was still there, looking shocked.

Nothing had been changing in how we'd been looking at each other.

She wasn't looking shocked: she was looking furious.

She was saying something.

"Okay?" she said.

She pointed down the hall.

"Go to your room."

—Stanley's Brother—

He took a half-day at work and drove the five hours from Chicago to Collinsville, and I got in the car, and he drove the five hours from Collinsville to Chicago.

"There's some sausage pizza in the cooler," he said. "From this new joint in my neighborhood, Slicer Miller's."

He ate a piece.

"They've got a kick-ass vegan pizza. I'm pretty skeptical of vegan 'cheese,' believe me, but dude, that pizza's good. I don't know how they do it! We should take Mom there sometime."

"Mom's a weekend vegan again," he explained.

He put on music.

He put on a comedy podcast.

He put on a history podcast.

After a while he said, "You punched somebody, didn't you."

—Stanley's Mom

My mom and I sat at the bar in the Chicago Brauhaus and waited for my brother to show up. We both knew that he was late on purpose.

He'd arranged the dinner, like usual. At first I'd said I wasn't sure I could make it.

"What if you come as a favor?" he'd said. "A favor to me, your brother. Who does you favors?"

Later that week, our mom was leaving for her annual summer trip to Europe.

She and I ordered drinks.

"This year I have a conference in Kraków," she said.

I asked her what the conference was about.

She told me.

The bartender brought two dimpled half-liters of bright beer.

"Na zdrowie," whispered my mom, raising her glass sneakily.

It'd been a week since I'd quit the dig. My thumb was in a splint. I'd told T everything that'd happened, except for the attempted kiss, and from this sparked a fight that hadn't ended, that'd flared and spat for seven days. T called my decision to leave Cahokia unacceptable. For her, it was as if I'd been cast in my dream show, only I hadn't been given my dream role,

I'd been given a challenging minor role, a character I wasn't immediately good at playing, and instead of buckling down after a failed first rehearsal, instead of grinding hard to come up with what it took to rise to the occasion of the role, I'd quit. T had said, No one who does that can work in theater! and I said, That's the point! and our fight, which had been about Caholtia, began to melt into other subjects—previous fights and complaints and issues—and my decision to quit the dig became a signifier for other actions and inactions, which brought us to how I'd announced my intent to propose, which brought us to how I'd admitted to having bought a ring, which brought us to what these facts revealed about the nature of our relationship. We fought in the apartment and on the street. We fought over text and through email. We improvised new ways to explain what we'd already explained, rehashing, replaying, redoing, and when something was said that set me off, I'd shout, This might be as "far" as we can "go"! and when something was said that set her off, she'd shout, How else do you become a "different person" but by taking "uncomfortable actions"! and my hands would clench, and my jaw would clamp, and I'd begin to be sure that at any moment a gash would tear open in my conscience out of which would gush an act of violence. T would leave for rehearsal in the high heat of one of the middles of our fight. The door would slam. I'd open our cabinet and pick a glass, a water glass or a beer glass or a wineglass, hers or mine. I'd stand with it. I'd see myself smashing it. I'd see myself throwing a plate and flipping a table and kicking a wall and punching a window and grabbing or pushing or slapping or striking T. I'd stop. Nausea would rock me. I'd be standing somewhere else, the glass in my hand—the bedroom, the hallway, the stairwell, the alley. I'd put the glass back. There'd been no work for me that week; I'd told Niko I'd be in Collinsville for the summer. He'd hired someone else. When T was at work or rehearsal, I sat on the couch, or under the red maple at Welles Park, or at the two-person tables in the Grind, the local coffee shop I liked, where the baristas, who recognized me, began to pretend they didn't.

My mom said, "I'm presenting a paper on immersive learning experiences."

We reached for our beers at the same time and drank from them with the same poky intentionality. We both moved a little like large domesticated animals. I resembled her, but sounded like my dad, and my brother resembled our dad, but sounded like our mom. It'd been that way since we were kids.

My mom looked like she usually did at the end of a semester: worn out and weary-eyed, but animated, already turning it around. A lightness lifted her. This was also how she looked when she was dating again, whether she'd gone back to my dad or was seeing someone new.

She waited for me to say something.

"Conferences are reunions," she said. "I can't wait to see my people."

A server brought us a pretzel.

The bar and the dining room shared the same space, which gave the restaurant the feel of a private club. On a small stage, a pair of handsome elderly German musicians in folk costumes performed, one on an electronic keyboard, the other on an ornate accordion. Both appeared to be wandering into pleasant imaginary worlds.

"The next song," said the keyboardist, "it is a song about a woman who is in love. She is very sad. She tells the world. Never before has there been such a song."

I did and didn't want to propose to T, and I knew I shouldn't, and I knew I would.

My mom said, "You're too private."

Torrentelli had said: Tell her true things!

"Things aren't good," I said.

"Oh yeah?"

"I keep doing the wrong thing."

"Like what."

I stared at my beer. "I tried to cheat on T."

"Does she know about it?"

"No."

"Do you know how many times I tried to cheat on your father?"

Our phones chimed, faceup on the bar—a text from my brother: Parking!

My mom turned on her bar stool to look me in the eye. Her face was wide and square, like mine, but her default expression was open.

Her openness shut.

"I need to tell you something, kiddo," she said.

At this moment I realized that she'd been drinking before we met at the bar.

"You're a reasonable person," she said, meaning, You need to start being more reasonable.

"You have a good heart," she said, meaning, You need to start thinking about other people.

"You're in your twenties," she said, meaning, You're a dupa jasiu.

"What is it," I said.

"You've got plenty of time to find what you love."

"Yes."

"I'm saying that you're right to walk away from whatever you need to walk away from. You get me?"

"You're telling me to break up with T."

She put her hand to her chest. "God no—I'm talking about archaeology, about how you left the excavation. I've only met the girl twice. I don't know anything about her, about you and her."

I looked away, at the stage, where the musicians were in the middle of another song. "I should," I said.

My mother touched my hand. "No, Stanley."

I was confused.

"Walk away from what you've got to walk away from, but with somebody you love, don't get hasty. You'll want to walk right back."

"T and me aren't you and Dad."

"That's not what I'm saying."

I asked her to say what she was saying.

She was holding my hand now.

She said, "You're a difficult person. You're a difficult person to love."

I took my hand away.

"It's all your brother and I—and your aunt, sometimes she calls me—talk about. How to get you to help yourself. You should hear us. It'd do you good."

I rose from my bar stool.

"That's a compliment!" she said, irritated. "Use your head. You think we don't have other things to talk about? You think if you're angry and bitter and touchy all the time, people are going to see through it to your sensitive side, and they'll admire you, like your private life is a movie everybody can watch?"

I walked out of the bar and through the dining room and into the hallway, where I passed my brother, who was rushing in, mid-text, who didn't see me, and it wasn't until I made it outside, by the brick wall entrance and the sidewalk sign of a doofy stein-wielding chef, that I saw that I hadn't let go of my beer glass.

Across the street, the fountain in the leafy plaza burbled. Moms and dads watched kids chase each other from bench to bench. An old man soloed on a clarinet. I leaned against the brick wall, which was warm, and chugged what was left of the beer. I'd always assumed it'd been my dad who'd kept coming back to my mom, every other year. Now I was sure that it was the other way around. I didn't want this to make me mad, but it did.

The door opened. A furious middle-aged bartender said, "You forget something?"

I stared at him.

He nodded. "Just give me back my glassware, asshole."

I unleaned from the wall.

"You gonna make me get it?" he said, straightening.

I turned the glass fist-wise, like it was a pair of brass knuckles.

The bartender twitched.

I punched the wall—the glass exploded.

PART III

LIFE IS BRUTAL
AND FULL OF TRAPS

Stanley Sits on a Cot in a Cell in the Dark

The space at the center of myself that wasn't me that had become me wasn't me anymore. I felt around for it, to make sure.
I was sure.

93

Stanley Sits on a Cot in a Cell in the Dark and Considers to What Degree His Having Been Wrong About Reading Faces Has Affected His Relationships with Family, Friends, and T

I took off my shoes. I took off my socks.

94

Stanley Sits on a Cot in a Cell in the Dark and Considers to What Degree His Decision to Knowingly but Unwillingly Agree to Involvement in a Personalized Performance Art Project in a Foreign Country Has Changed His Self-Conception

Pipes trickled and drained, clogged.
    Springs in the mattress crunched.
    An exit sign buzzed.

Stanley Sits on a Cot in a Cell in the Dark and Considers Whether or Not His Decision to Knowingly but Unwillingly Agree to Involvement in a Personalized Performance Art Project in a Foreign Country Has Accelerated Changes in His Self-Conception That He Would Have Come to Anyway, on His Own, Alone

I scooted, to sit cross-legged.

Stanley Sits on a Cot in a Cell in the Dark and Tries to Remember When He's Felt This Way Before

The air was close and old.

Stanley Sits on a Cot in a Cell in the Dark and
Remembers the Time in High School After Class
in the Parking Lot When He Was Walking Around
Looking for Torrentelli or Barton or Torrentelli's Car,
and at the End of the Lot He Found Marcus Svachma
and Ronan O'Kelly Up in Torrentelli's Face, Calling
Him a Fag and a Freak, and Stanley Approached,
and They Called Stanley a Fag and a Freak and a
Fuckup, and Stanley Called Them Fascists, and as
They Moved Step-by-Step into the Fight That None
of Them Had It in Them at That Time in Their Lives to
Avoid, Part of Stanley Realized That Through These
Exchanges Marcus Svachma and Ronan O'Kelly Were
Co-creating a Woefully Reductive Misconception
of Stanley, a Misconception That Stanley Perhaps
Encouraged (or at the Very Least Failed to
Discourage) Through How He Acted (Misanthropic
Anger, Existential Apathy, Pessimism, Privilege) and
What He Wore (Trench Coats, Explicit T-Shirts That
Teachers Made Him Turn Inside Out, Baggy Jeans,
Dog Collars, Black Lipstick, Red Contact Lenses), and
Although This Was True, at the Same Time, Stanley
and Torrentelli Were Co-creating Woefully Reductive
Misconceptions of Marcus Svachma and Ronan
O'Kelly, Misconceptions That Marcus Svachma and
Ronan O'Kelly Without a Doubt Encouraged Through
How They Acted (Antagonistic Anger, Academic
Apathy, Pessimism, Privilege) and What They Wore
(Designer Casual, Designer Sportswear), and This
Realization of His Accountability in a System of Two-
Way Misrepresentation Was What Stanley Struggled
with but Didn't Mention During His Three-Day Hospital
Stay and Three-Week School Suspension When He

Argued with His Dad, Mom, and Brother About Who He Was and Wasn't, with His Dad Saying That If It Walks Like a Freak and Talks Like a Freak It's a Freak, with His Mom Saying That Yes, She Agreed That He Knew Who He Was, It Was Just That He Had to Figure Out How to Be Himself About It, and with His Brother Saying That Although It Might Not Seem Possible Now, Before He Knew It He Wouldn't Be Able to Equate the Way He Dressed and Acted with Who He Was, Even If He Wanted to, Ever Again

I was closing my eyes.

Then I was opening them: I was lying on the cot.

I sat up. I was sitting on the cot. I was sitting on the edge of the cot.

I was closing my eyes again.

I was dragging myself through dreams or dreams were dragging me through myself.

Then I was opening my eyes again: I opened my eyes again:

Stanley Is Released

A lawyer from the embassy who looked like a lawyer from the embassy met me in a room outside the cell in the police station in the morning. I didn't know how to read her face.

"Do you understand what I'm saying to you?" she was saying.

We were sitting at a table.

She was saying that the man I'd assaulted, a Polish citizen, had declined to press charges.

I was filling out forms. There was hot coffee.

Then we were sitting at a different table in a different room with two different police officers who looked like two different police officers.

I was signing forms, I was paying a fine.

Then I was saying, "Where can I make a call."

The lawyer was saying that she had just said where.

"You did," I said.

I remembered that she'd told me but I didn't remember what she'd said.

I said this to her.

"No," I said to her suggestions.

I was jammed in a doorway in myself. I couldn't enter, I couldn't exit. No one was getting through, not family, not friends, not strangers.

The lawyer gave me her card.

Phones blooped.

I was in a hallway, at a bank of pay phones.

I called my brother. My father answered.

"What," he said. "Who is this?"

I hadn't dialed my brother's number: I'd dialed my father's number.

"Stanley?" said my father.

He sounded afraid but I couldn't be sure.

"Get out of there," he said.

I was outside. Rain was falling. Rain was falling out of itself and into itself, falling in shining blades, falling in a slashing and a toppling, falling in a sparkling-edged tumbling. I stood in it. It didn't make sense. I continued to miss things—impressions, connections, instructions, conclusions. I couldn't read faces. In the time when I'd thought I could read faces, I couldn't. I couldn't think straight and I didn't feel solid. Things happened slow and then things happened fast. My shirt and jeans tightened, soaked. What I wanted was to wreck the performance art project, to destroy my uncle's cameras and cell phones and computers, to incapacitate my uncle and the artists with painful bodily injuries. What I knew, however, was that any actions I took to attempt to achieve these goals would provide my uncle and the artists with more material. They'd already accumulated enough to produce a collage-like installation of images and artifacts, as they'd done with *Country-Western Country* and the pissing politicians project, an installation that could present me as any sort of person, that could open at a Chicago art gallery, that could begin with the surprise photo taken of me by my uncle in his bathroom on my aunt's birthday, that could peak with video of my reactions to yesterday's reenacted proposal in Old Town Square, and that could conclude with an image yet to be captured of me walking out of my uncle's apartment with my bag.

On the phone I'd told my father I was coming home.

"Good," he said.

"Is T okay?" he said.

T doesn't need your help, I said to myself.

Rain pinged and plunked and splashed.

Near a tram station I stopped at a tourist information booth. Behind its foggy glass sat a tourist agent who looked like a tourist agent. She took off her tourist agent glasses. She lowered the book she was reading. On its cover was an image of a spooky egg.

I said, "How do I get to Old Town Square."

She waited. I couldn't read her face.

I opened my mouth to repeat myself, and she interrupted me to say, "Good afternoon."

I looked around at the afternoon: gray, wet, gleaming.

Then she said, "Excuse me. Pardon me."

I said that she hadn't done anything wrong yet.

"Please exercise basic courtesies before imposing your information requests on public servants, or anyone else, especially when you are imposing these requests in a foreign language."

I asked if there was somebody in the booth I could talk to who wasn't her.

She picked up her book.

The rain intensified, falling all over itself.

People shuffled umbrellas up and down in passing.

I stood under an awning and listened to the rain, and I stood under an alley archway and smelled the rain, and I stood in the open on a corner and felt the rain.

The rain changed its mind: it fell casually.

I stumbled, tripped, and slid on crushed cobblestones, on loose and missing cobblestones, on perfect cobblestones.

Trams whooshed by.

Men and women ran to cars.

On a coned-off street, under tents, in two kinds of light, a film crew worked. The lights that were there to light the scene and the lights that were there to light the set carved separate colors and shapes, one blue and broad, for the actors, one white and narrow, for the crew. In the first light, a woman who looked like a director went over a clipboard with a woman who looked like a cinematographer about what they were to do now that the rain had changed its mind. In the other light, two women who looked like actors stood under the same umbrella and shared the same cigarette, passing it back and forth, not speaking. One of the smoking women was T.

A woman in a reflective poncho stopped me from getting close.

I said that I knew one of the actors.

She shook her head.

I said that I was an actor.

"No English," she said.

I sidestepped her—I went past the cones and up to a sawhorse, near the lights.

"T," I said.

She yawned.

I shouted and waved.

T turned into a woman who looked like T.

"No," said the woman in the poncho, in front of me again. She gestured me away: "Goodbye, goodbye."

The woman who looked like T turned into a woman who didn't look like T.

Stay away, I said to myself.

I turned a corner and collided with a man. We fell. He rushed to his feet, flailing and hollering, and I rushed to mine, fists balled, and as he scrambled, he whipped his umbrella in front of him in such a way that when I rose I stepped right into it with my face. A tine touched my eye, then untouched it. I clapped my hand to my face and screamed. The man froze. I snatched his umbrella and broke it over my knee.

He kept still, hands up.

I was running in an alley and shouting.

The alley was shouting back—shouting echoes, shouting shadows.

A hot coil of pain uncurled in my eye.

I was in another alley.

I was on a corner, bent, huffing.

Then I was at the door to a bar. I was in the bar, waiting. There were two long communal tables loaded up with men. All of the men drank, some of the men ate. Many flipped through newspapers or scrolled through phones. The men were my age, middle-aged, and old. They took turns talking. I stared at them, one by one: they all looked like themselves, like they could never not be themselves, here or in any other place, with each other or alone. I didn't need to know how to read their faces to know that they belonged to where they were. Where they were was with themselves.

A server sat me between two men who looked like brothers.

My beard dripped. Puddles sponged out of me, onto the table, the bench, the floor. I hadn't let go of the busted umbrella.

The man to my left, wearing a suit but no tie, scooted away. He made a face.

If I didn't blink my hurt eye it didn't hurt.

A beer and a ticket appeared.

I closed my good eye and looked through the hurt one: a killing haze.

"American?" said the man to my right, who also wore a suit but no tie.

I said I was from Chicago.

The man to my left got up with a grunt. He closed his newspaper, tossed it to a man across the table, and left.

"America," said the man to my right. "One time I go. No more."

I finished my beer, put it down, and touched at my face.

"You are good?" said the man to my right, motioning at his own eye.

My empty glass had been replaced by a full glass.

"You have family?" said the man to my right. "Czech Republic? You look."

"Poland," I said. "Polish. Polack."

He chuckled. "Yes, Polack is illegal."

"Kraków is best," said a man on his way out.

A new man sat to my left, wearing a blazer and sweater. He looked at me, and then at the jar of food in front of him, and then at me. He said something.

Men across the table looked up from conversations and newspapers and phones.

The new man to my left repeated himself.

Everyone laughed.

The man to my right pointed at the new man's jar. "Utopenci. You understand utopenci?"

He tried to translate.

A man across the table tried to help him.

A different man, one I couldn't see, said, "Drown."

"Drowned!" said the man across the table, clapping once.

The man across the table was the made-up man.

"Drowned man!" he said, smiling.

I was on my feet—my chair crashed to the floor.

"Drowned men," said the man to my right, picking up my chair, touching my elbow. "Utopenci is drowned men." He mimed water dripping from his body, he mimed a dead face. "You are utopenci!"

"Joke," said the made-up man.

The made-up man turned into a man who looked like the made-up man.

I sat. A jar of utopenci appeared in front of me: fat pickled sausages packed in a brine with onions, sauerkraut, spices.

"Good?" said the man who looked like the made-up man.

Another beer.

The man to my left examined my umbrella, flexing it.

I blinked my hurt eye: a jagged heat.

A beer.

"You are visit?" said the man to my right.

"Yes."

"Why?"

I said that I wanted to be the kind of man who would go to a place for a woman.

He didn't understand.

"I am here to see a woman," I said.

The man who looked like the made-up man tried to translate.

"A woman!" said the man to my right. "Yes. Good."

He clacked glasses with me.

"Where is a woman?" he said.

I was weeping.

None of the men were talking and then all of the men were talking.

I was saying, "What time is it."

I was saying, "Thank you."

I was saying, "No thanks."

I was outside and walking, and no rain was falling, and the sky was jumping with sideways lightning, with crooked bolts branching and breaking and burning and dying, and black clouds were flashing blue, and no thunder was following the lightning, and at every intersection I was seeing where I was.

The men had drawn me a map on a napkin.

"You," they'd said, marking an X.

"Call me," the lawyer from the embassy had said.

"There is nothing," Information had said, leaving.

"You're afraid," I'd said to my father.

He said he was.

He said, "He can't make you do anything you don't want to do."

A street I hadn't been on shunted me into an Old Town Square I didn't recognize. It'd been unpacked of people. A man leaned on the green monument, staring straight up at the sky, and two women hovered at the clock tower, taking pictures of it from different distances. Pitted dips in the cobblestones pooled water and streetlight.

More lightning opened.

No thunder closed.

I unlocked the door to the apartment building. On the lobby wall was a chalk drawing of a man punching another man. Both of the men were me. I wiped them into blurs with the broken umbrella. On the staircase wall was another chalk drawing, this one of me behind bars, only every bar was also me, a sequence of me's, bar-shaped and -sized. I couldn't read my faces. I smudged them, caking the umbrella's canopy in chalk paste. On the door to the apartment I'd been staying in was one more drawing: an over-the-shoulder perspective of me pushing open a door. Through the opening in the depicted door a woman in a dress waited with her back turned. Most of her was in view, but only a third of what should have been visible had been drawn—the lines of the woman's side broke off unfinished, her figure abandoned. Enough of her was there to see that she was T. I didn't erase her. I opened the door.

The man who was meant to be me, the one I'd right-hooked in Old Town Square, sat at the table, his face battered. With one hand he read *Sacred Centers*. With the other he pointed a revolver at Manny.

Manny sat at the other end of the table, his hands on his roller bag. One of the lenses of his glasses was cracked. A welt rose from his forehead, where I'd smacked him with the shoe.

It took him a moment to speak.

"There is blood in your eye," he said.

The man who was meant to be me said, "What do I want to know."

His voice growled out in a gritty imitation of mine.

"Would you please, please, please instruct this man to put his firearm away?" said Manny.

I walked past them to the bathroom, where I peeled off my

shirt, underwear, jeans, and socks. I changed into clean, dry clothes: slacks and a dress shirt. My hurt eye was blood-sodden, the bottom quarter red-brown. Its blinking lagged. I touched my beard, its knots and tangles, its crusted puke. Everything stank. I uncapped my electric razor. I buzzed off my beard, layer by layer, cutting close. Hair piled in the sink.

I washed my bare face.

I brushed my teeth.

I applied deodorant.

I wrung out my wet clothes and wrapped them in a towel.

I repacked my bag.

At the couch I opened my laptop. The webcam winked on, live.

"Stanley?" said Manny.

"What do I want to know about what else is planned," said the man who was meant to be me.

I opened my browser. There were emails from Torrentelli and Barton and my brother and my mother, all of them in response to emails they'd received from my account, emails I hadn't written or sent myself, and there were three emails from myself to myself, titled "DAY ONE PLOT" through "DAY THREE PLOT," each with an attachment, and there were two emails from T, sent on their own, not in response to anything. I deleted every one of them unread. I closed my bad eye and focused on the screen and wrote to my brother: I went to Kutná Hora, thank you; I didn't see a shadow puppet sex show; I ate a fried cheese sandwich and then another fried cheese sandwich and at the time it was what I wanted, thank you; I didn't contact Mom and I won't; T and I are through; I can no longer pretend to know people's feelings and thoughts and motivations based on what I see in their faces; I want to go back to the beginning of myself; you can't go back to the beginning of yourself.

"Please help me," said Manny.

I sent the email. I opened the window and let the laptop drop onto the street.

I went to the kitchen table. Manny looked at me, and then at the man who was meant to be me, and then at me. The man's beard, which had been a copy of mine, had disappeared. He was clean-shaven.

I tugged *Sacred Centers* out of his hand and stuffed it in my bag.

He kept the gun on Manny.

"You have no intention of helping," said Manny to me. He turned to the man who was meant to be me and said, "Stanley has arrived—here is your man. May I now go?"

The man said, "What do I want to know about what else is planned for me in this performance."

"You're involved," I said to Manny.

"*The Made-Up Man*," said the man to me.

"You're not a victim," I said.

"He's not the made-up man," said the man.

Manny jumped to his feet, upsetting his roller bag.

The man adjusted his aim accordingly.

"I am involved *and* I am a victim!" said Manny.

"I don't respect you," I said.

"He has no character," said the man who was meant to be me.

Manny glanced at the door. He glanced at the gun.

"I signed no nondisclosure agreement," he said.

He explained that my uncle had approached him through social media and offered him five hundred euros for each night he stayed in the apartment, with the opportunity for two hundred and fifty more per ad hoc request. My uncle had required that Manny ask T to ask me to put him up, which, at the time, seemed permissible. Despite what Manny had read about my uncle's reputation (violations of privacy, injury and wrongful death lawsuits, suspicion of criminal involvement in Eastern

European illegal immigration networks, subsequent exploitation of illegal immigrants), he agreed, he arrived, he endured my idiocy, abuse, and denial (I should see a therapist immediately, he'd never met a man so unaware of himself). He saw fit to accept a number of ad hoc requests (taking me out to a restaurant to ask me about graduate school and employment, taking me on a walk to offer me an unsolicited assessment of the nature of my relationship with T), attempted but aborted another (taking me out to a café to ask me about my mother and my father and my brother and my aunt), and rejected several appalling ones (telling me the story of how he recovered from his first breakup, telling me the story of how he recovered from his worst breakup, giving me a hug).

"Do you understand why I am providing you with this information?" said Manny.

I nodded. "You're not important."

"This is not his story," said the man who was meant to be me.

Manny went on: after I walloped him with the shoe and rampaged out, that was it, he'd decided to end the business relationship. Before he finished packing, though, he was approached by a preposterously dressed woman who sang instead of speaking, who introduced herself as "Mystery." Mystery offered Manny twice the nightly rate to remain in the apartment until I returned. Manny refused. Mystery upped the offer to five times the rate. Manny asked for ten.

"With that revealed, I know what conclusion you've come to," said Manny. "That is why I want you to listen closely: no sum, however high, could make me execute a request detrimental to T."

He cited turned-down requests to invite T to the restaurant, on the walk, and to the apartment.

"That is why I am here," he said. "I could not rely on you to keep her out of it."

I put down my bag.

Manny drew a breath.

I took the gun from the man's hand—he didn't resist—I stepped back and pointed it at the floor.

"Go," I said to Manny.

He snatched an envelope off the table, one I hadn't seen, and tore it open to a bundle of rubber-banded cash. "You must know that what you have done—what you are doing—is irresponsible and selfish," he said.

He counted the bills, quick as a banker.

"When I arrived, T sent me many texts," he said. "She hoped to meet the both of us for a coffee. She hoped to visit us here, in this apartment."

He opened the door, looked both ways.

"Would you consider me 'important,' would you 'respect' me," he said, "if I told you how I persuaded her to keep away?"

"You don't love her any more than I do," I said.

"He might," said the man.

Manny did a little air hump.

"I informed her of your attempt to place your dick in your professor."

He slammed the door behind him.

"Unfaithful! Desperate! Unimaginative!" he screamed.

My mother had told my aunt, I realized, and my aunt had told my uncle, and my uncle had told whoever he'd needed to tell to achieve whatever he'd needed to achieve.

Manny's roller bag bumped down the hall.

"And you, 'artists,' hear me! I am not prohibited from reporting your activities to the authorities!"

His roller bag clabbered on the steps.

"Arrest! Incarceration! Litigation!"

The lobby door shut with a whump.

The man who was meant to be me looked me in the eye.

"I'm not sure who I am," he said.

"You're a performance artist!" I yelled.

I sounded but didn't feel drunk.

He looked straight ahead. His posture loosened.

"Perform!" I said.

"I've been thinking about something my uncle said to me at my aunt's birthday party," he said. "He sat me down at the breakfast bar. He had a proposal. He said that I was the man for it because I was 'actual.' He said that I know why I take the actions that I take."

He opened a tin case of hand-rolled cigarettes.

"I've been thinking about this idea a lot," he said. "I've been thinking about it even when I didn't know that I was thinking about it. It's because I want to believe it. It's a view of myself that's easy."

He checked both sides of the cigarette and then he put it in his mouth.

He said, "It's clear to me now that my uncle said this only because he believes the opposite to be true, that I don't know why I take the actions that I take. That my view of myself is made up."

He offered me a cigarette. I tucked it into my shirt pocket.

"I've been thinking about my father," he said, closing the tin case. "My father is an American man. He tells himself, and others, that he's the kind of man who says what he means and means what he says. That he's a mystery he's solved."

He searched himself for a lighter.

"I don't want to admit it, but I try to be like my father. I'm trying to believe, for example, that I came to Prague because of a woman."

Someone in the hallway sighed.

"Because of the idea of a woman," he said.

Someone in the hallway sighed differently.

"I've been thinking about my aunt," he said. "My aunt is an American woman."

He was doing an impression of my heaped-forward way of sitting, of my leg-bopping. But without the beard, his bruised face was his, not mine, and his antihero growl registered nowhere near my voice. There was something else: lodged in his ear was a wireless earpiece.

He found a lighter.

I plucked the earpiece out. His talking stopped; he put down his props.

From the earpiece came a voice.

The voice was my uncle's.

My uncle was saying, "I am trying to believe, for example, that I am coming to Prague because of myself, because of the idea of myself."

He stopped, waiting.

I moved close to the man who was meant to be me. I held the earpiece between us, so that the both of us could listen, and I said, "I hear you."

My uncle said, "I am understanding the project now."

The man who was meant to be me said, "I understand the project now."

My uncle said, "I am understanding the origin now, the motive of my uncle and my aunt, it is in me now, I am seeing it, I am re-seeing it: there is worry about me. My aunt hears worry from my brother and from my mother, and she goes to T, she hears worry from T. She thinks. She goes to the garage, to the workshop, to my uncle, she says, 'We must help Stasiu. Let Stasiu be the one to help with art. Let Stasiu be the one to help with what is next.' And my uncle, he is working, he is working on the film noir and the detective novel and the crime mystery and the thriller, and America, always America, the shining surface of America, he is working on a project of a scale of which he has but dreamed, of a mode of great darkness and truth, a project that is to be a living shadow of a life, an actual life, close to it, cast by it, and he says to my aunt, 'I love you.' They plan together. They plan to make me the made-up man. My uncle plans plot, my aunt plans the proposal that my uncle will give to me. They plan the parts in secret, not sharing: this is my uncle's condition. My aunt's condition: 'It must help him.'

They are working. My aunt, she is working, she is working like she has not worked since marriage. It is renewal. The day my uncle is to offer the proposal to me, the day of my aunt's birthday, they share, they review. My aunt is broken into horror. She says, 'This is destructive, this is not instructive.' 'Destructive is instructive,' says my uncle. They fight. The fight is old and bad, but new and worse, and family, and my aunt says if the plot does not change, she will not betray the project but she will move out, she will never return, she will bring heartbreak to herself and to my uncle. I am understanding now: this is the most important moment for my uncle. This is the moment of great darkness and truth. He re-sees. He re-sees the why of how previous projects, *Country-Western Country* and *O Say Can You Pee*, failed. You do not instruct the community, such as America, by instructing the community, such as country-western music. You instruct the community by instructing the individual. And you must use the community, all of the community, to instruct the individual . . ."

At almost the same time, with a delayed overlap, as if translating, the man who was meant to be me was saying, ". . . I understand the origin of the project now. Everyone was worried about me. My aunt went to my family, she went to T, she listened. No one could help. She thought about it. She went to my uncle, who was working on a project, his most ambitious to date, a shadow-project—"

I pulled away from the man, keeping the earpiece.

My uncle said, "My uncle says, 'Action is not a shadow made by man! Man is a shadow made by action!'"

I threw down the earpiece and stomped it.

The man who was meant to be me didn't react.

I screamed that this wasn't canvases or clay, this was people, people whether or not they'd been paid, whether or not they were in the know, this was despicable, this was unethical, this wasn't being artists, this was being criminals.

"I'm sorry I hit you," I said to the man.

"I can stop," I said.

"You," I said. "You can stop."

"I made a mistake," said the man, still imitating me.

He did a face that I pretended to read: me beginning to swerve away from myself.

I flipped the table—it cracked to its side on the floor.

"I shouldn't have come," he said.

I tapped the gun against my leg.

Sweat poured from all parts of the man's face.

"Why do you think you know how to be me?" I said.

He looked at his hands. "I don't know what I'll do next."

I thought about what my uncle would want me to do next, which was any action that would artistically enrich *The Made-Up Man*, and what my aunt would want me to do next, which was access another way of seeing things, and what my dad would want me to do next, which was leave, and what my mom would want me to do next, which was grow up, and what my brother would want me to do next, which was be my best self, a self just outside and above the borders of my ordinary everyday sum-average self, a self to push for, and what T would want me to do next, which was I didn't know what because the T I'd known since she'd moved out was a T I'd imagined.

"You'll talk to me about it," said a woman in a dress in the doorway.

It was the made-up woman. She was now meant to be T.

"There's still time," she said.

Her dress was one that T would wear, bright and classy, and her hair was done like T's, down and dark and wavy, and her voice was like T's when T spoke in the voice of the character she played in *Black and White and Dead All Over*.

"I'm here," she said.

I shut the door on her and locked it, and I grabbed the man who was meant to be me by the shoulder and yanked him backwards. He slammed to the floor, flat on the back of the chair. I planted my foot on his face. He squirmed—I pressed his cheek, pinning his head to one side. I pointed the gun at my foot on his face.

He stopped moving.

I fired—I fired all six rounds—every one a booming blank.

The man rolled, hands on his ears, grimacing.

My hearing hummed and popped. I stepped back, I waved smoke.

The man wasn't grimacing. He was grinning.

I clubbed him in the head with the gun. He threw up his hands. I circled, to find an opening, and I clubbed him again. He tried to get up and couldn't. Then I wasn't sure if what I'd seen was a grin or a grimace, the prelude to laughter or to pain, and I stopped, embarrassed and outraged, and I might have clubbed him again but the woman who was meant to be T was at my side, keys in hand, wrenching me by the arm.

She looked like T, she smelled like T.

The gun fell out of my hand.

She was speaking.

Blood was welling from above the man's ear.

The man and the woman were speaking Polish.

We were lifting the man to his feet.

We were walking the man down the stairwell.

We were walking the man through the alley to the street.

We were helping the man into a cab.

"I am acting," the man was saying.

The cab left.

There was lightning.

The woman kept her hand on my arm. "I am no longer acting, okay?"

I went inside for my bag and she followed.

There was no one on the stairs or in the hallway or in the apartment.

"Do not leave me here," she said.

I went outside with my bag and she followed.

There was no one in the alley or in the street.

"I am coming with you, let me come with you."

I waited for a cab.

"Listen," she said. "I am not going to act, I don't want to, but if I stay with you, Lech is going to pay me more, he wants me to stay with you. Allow me. Just please do not hurt me, okay?"

A cab pulled up.

"Okay," said the woman.

She was trembling.

I got in the cab and said, "Airport."

"Airport," said the driver.

The woman who was meant to be T tried to scoot in beside me but I blocked her.

"No!" she screamed, shoving me, striking me, "my family, my family!"

I closed the door on her again.

"I'm helping her," I said to the cabbie.

The cabbie pulled up to the curb at Departures.

I didn't get out of the car.

The cabbie opened the door for me. "Airport," he said.

I showed him the ticket to T's play.

The cabbie pulled up to the curb at the theater.

In the lobby the lights dipped, dimming and undimming, the end of intermission. I stood still. Audience members glimmered. They drank and chatted, herding. Some wore dresses and suits and ties, some wore what looked like costumes, outfits and wigs and masks. I followed them into the house, toward the seats, but an usher stopped me at the entrance and asked to see my ticket. I stepped aside to go through my pockets.

Afiya passed, laughing, surrounded by middle-aged men and women.

There was no ticket. I bought another at the box office.

"What show are you in?" said the usher.

I didn't understand.

"Your makeup," she said, pointing at my eye.

I was seated in the front row, far left. I waved my hand in front of my face. I'd stopped being able to see out of my hurt eye.

The lights went out, the curtains went up.

The behind-the-scenes set of an old-time radio drama: a booth, a table and chairs, microphones and scripts. Jazz played, low and rich and dangerous. The edges of instruments sparkled in the pit. In the Chicago production, the intros and outros had all been canned.

The live music lifted me a little outside of myself.

I floated in the dark.

T wasn't in the second act until halfway through it.

The actors entered, lit.

I gathered in myself: I found that I could read the actors' faces. T had told me about objectives. In this production, every actor's every action was supported by a simple clear intention, a moment-by-moment motivation. Find a secret. Hide a lie. Kill an anger. Induce a love. Some of these objectives were worked out ahead of time with the help of the director. Some of these objectives were improvised onstage, grounded in an actor's intellectual or emotional understanding of a character. All of these objectives, for as knowable as they were on their own, created mystery when they were put together. You don't always see them, T had said. But they're there.

I saw them.

T entered, her character fake-aloof.

She said her line but I didn't hear it. I only saw her.

There was laughter and applause. She was a favorite.

Her character had come from the scene of an accident that would turn out to have been on purpose. Her dress was rumpled, her scarf was stained.

"You don't say," she said.

She took her spot at the table in the radio booth. She glanced at her script. She put on lipstick. Other actors were talking.

One actor, playing the producer, slapped down a letter, a complaint from a listener who called T's character's character unlikable and unrealistic.

T gestured indifferently at the audience, started to say her line, and saw me in my seat.

She paused. A stricken, painful, shaken pause.

The audience tipped into it. Everyone was with her.

This wasn't how she'd been playing this moment but I saw that this was how she'd have to play it from then on. The actor playing the producer sat, surprised.

T remembered who she was supposed to be.

T remembered who the who she was being was trying to be.

She said her line: "You try being somebody nobody expects to be complex."

I was getting up.

I was bumping legs, I was stepping on shoes.

I was outside.

The cabbie was standing at his cab, smoking.

"Your bag," he said.

I'd left it in the backseat.

I was in the backseat, smoking.

"Airport," I said.

The cabbie pulled up to the curb at a hospital.

He opened the door for me.

Stanley Is Treated

I was in wide light on a gurney in the ER and I was in wide light on a bed in a room.

My eye was bandaged shut.

In a bed beside me lounged a teenager. Half of his head had been shaved and stitched. He ate sausages out of a bag and watched the TV on the wall.

He watched Czech game shows; he watched Czech news.

He said something to himself every now and again.

I steeped in meds.

On the news appeared an insert of an image of my uncle's face. The image wasn't recent. Then a shot of his apartment building, with squad cars at the curb. Then footage of an interview with my uncle from what looked like ten years ago. He was angry.

I slept and I woke up and I slept.

What was happening was that parts of myself were going away. They were going away gradually. I didn't know the names of these parts, or what their dimensions were, or where and how they fit with other parts, but as soon as they were gone, it was as if they'd never been around to begin with. They didn't appear to be necessary.

For example, part of me wanted to be with T, to find T, to see T, to talk to T. Then that part of me went away. I thought that I would want that part of myself back, but I didn't, and then I thought that I would at least want to want it back, but I didn't. And yet I was still myself.

Between these parts was whatever was me, I concluded.

I felt variations of this feeling for a while.

Then I felt terror—cold and crushing—piling up, piling under—and I passed out.

Then I came back to another part of myself going away.

Then it repeated.

An old nurse said, "There is a visitor to see you."

I said that I wasn't seeing visitors.

The teenager in the bed next to mine read a book. He didn't look at me.

He read a different book.

"You will not be able to see out of your eye for likely forever," said a young doctor.

"I waited too long," I said.

"Correct," said the old nurse.

I signed papers, I received prescriptions.

"No flights for one week," said the old nurse.

I stepped into the hall, where there was no one I recognized, and then into the street, where there was no one I recognized.

I took a cab to a pharmacy and then to the train station.

"Poland," I said. "Polska."

The agent gave me a ticket for Kraków.

I pushed it back. "Warszawa."

Stanley Arrives in Warsaw

On the train my bag was stolen.

I took a cab to Old Town Market Square. The space was small and still, boxed in by shoved-together buildings. There was the feeling of a silenced folktale. At the center of the Square stood a statue of a naked mermaid, pushing out of a wave, gripping a sword and shield.

I walked until I found a hotel, where I reserved a room for a week. At the computer in the lobby I paid to change my return flight from going out of Prague to going out of Warsaw. I made a new email account—I told my brother and my father that I'd be back, but I didn't tell them where I was.

I plucked a tourist pamphlet out of a stand.

I went to a castle, I went to a palace, I went to a monument. I went to a restaurant and I went to a bar. I spoke the lines of Polish that I knew. I expected to see flashes of my family in the local men and women—Busia and Dziadzia's glares and frowns, my father's walk, my mother's voice. I expected to come to an understanding, or to touch a meaning, or to otherwise discover that I had the ability to make something out of being there.

I bought a bag and a set of clothes.

I didn't buy smokes.

I went on a walking tour, one that began in Old Town

Market Square. The guide said that only two of the buildings that surrounded the Square were originals. The rest were reconstructions of originals that had been systematically annihilated.

"The history of this city is the history of Poland," she said. "And Poland's history is the history of Europe. And Europe's history is the history of the West."

"Americans, are you listening?" she said.

The tour ended in a bar, with one free beer.

I drank a Lezajsk and ate lard spread.

The tour guide asked me where I was from.

"I have worked in Chicago," she said. "When I would meet Polish Americans, they would ask me where I was from. I would tell them. They would say, 'I would like to go to Warsaw.' And I would say, 'Do not go to Warsaw. Go to Kraków.'"

"I did not guess that you were American," she said.

I asked her why was that.

"I will not tell."

I asked her for her email.

She wrote it on the back of her tour company card. "I am older than you," she said.

I went to the Warsaw Uprising Museum, and the Museum of the History of Polish Jews, and the Polish History Museum, and the Warsaw Museum of Modern Art.

I went to the National Museum of Archaeology.

I peeled the bandage off of my eye. I turned to a mirror: my eye was pink and glazed. It looked like it was being regrown.

I tried to find an eye patch but couldn't. Nobody stared.

I went to a bookstore and I went to a park.

If the locals smiled, it seemed to be because they were sharing jokes about how little they smiled.

What the tour guide had written was unreadable.

One night I sat outside at a restaurant in the Square. The waiter, a man my age, recognized me from the night before, and brought me a vodka. There weren't many people out, in the Square itself and at the restaurants, but when they passed each other, they stopped to talk. It was the weekend. Lights and voices were low. My flight back was a day away: I would see Chicago from the window of a plane. I would walk through O'Hare to the Blue Line, and ride the Blue Line to the Lawrence bus, and ride the Lawrence bus to my apartment. I would turn on my phone to texts and voice mails.

Or I would skip my flight and find work in Warsaw. I would move into an apartment, work as many jobs as I could for as long as I was allowed, learn the language, and make something, I didn't know what, out of being there.

I ordered another vodka.

The waiter brought two and shot one with me.

"Na zdrowie," we said.

He pointed behind me and said something I didn't understand.

At the end of the Square, a horse-drawn carriage clunked up to a gathering of other horse-drawn carriages, the drivers on break.

The waiter smiled and went inside.

As I watched the men, I noticed that I'd started to see out of my bad eye, a little.

Shapes and shadows. Outlines, movement.

I didn't want to count on this. I focused on the men. One would speak, and the others would shake their heads. They all took a turn, their gestures brief and certain. Then they settled into a solid quiet. I waited for them to start over, but they didn't. They were done.

List of Scenes

85. —What Is Known About the Man Who'd Been Buried Without His Head—
86. —What Is Not—
87. —Dig—
88. —Ears Covered, Eyes Closed—an Artist—
89. —the End of the Dig—
90. —Stanley's Brother—
91. —Stanley's Mom
92. Stanley Sits on a Cot in a Cell in the Dark
93. Stanley Sits on a Cot in a Cell in the Dark and Considers to What Degree His Having Been Wrong About Reading Faces Has Affected His Relationships with Family, Friends, and T
94. Stanley Sits on a Cot in a Cell in the Dark and Considers to What Degree His Decision to Knowingly but Unwillingly Agree to Involvement in a Personalized Performance Art Project in a Foreign Country Has Changed His Self-Conception
95. Stanley Sits on a Cot in a Cell in the Dark and Considers Whether or Not His Decision to Knowingly but Unwillingly Agree to Involvement in a Personalized Performance Art Project in a Foreign Country Has Accelerated Changes in His Self-Conception That He Would Have Come to Anyway, on His Own, Alone
96. Stanley Sits on a Cot in a Cell in the Dark and Tries to Remember When He's Felt This Way Before
97. Stanley Sits on a Cot in a Cell in the Dark and Remembers the Time in High School After Class in the Parking Lot When He Was Walking Around Looking for Torrentelli or Barton or Torrentelli's Car, and at the End of the Lot He Found Marcus Svachma and Ronan O'Kelly Up in Torrentelli's Face, Calling Him a Fag and a Freak, and Stanley Approached, and They Called Stanley a Fag and a Freak and a Fuckup, and Stanley Called Them Fascists, and as They Moved Step-by-Step into the Fight That None of Them Had It in Them at That Time in Their Lives to Avoid, Part of Stanley Realized That Through These Exchanges Marcus Svachma and Ronan O'Kelly Were Co-creating a Woefully Reductive Misconception of Stanley, a Misconception That Stanley Perhaps Encouraged (or at the Very Least Failed to Discourage) Through How He Acted (Misanthropic Anger, Existential Apathy, Pessimism, Privilege) and What He Wore (Trench Coats, Explicit T-Shirts That Teachers Made Him Turn Inside Out, Baggy Jeans, Dog Collars, Black Lipstick, Red Contact Lenses), and Although This Was True, at the Same Time, Stanley and Torrentelli Were Co-creating Woefully Reductive Misconceptions of Marcus Svachma

and Ronan O'Kelly, Misconceptions That Marcus Svachma and Ronan O'Kelly Without a Doubt Encouraged Through How They Acted (Antagonistic Anger, Academic Apathy, Pessimism, Privilege) and What They Wore (Designer Casual, Designer Sportswear), and This Realization of His Accountability in a System of Two-Way Misrepresentation Was What Stanley Struggled with but Didn't Mention During His Three-Day Hospital Stay and Three-Week School Suspension When He Argued with His Dad, Mom, and Brother About Who He Was and Wasn't, with His Dad Saying That If It Walks Like a Freak and Talks Like a Freak It's a Freak, with His Mom Saying That Yes, She Agreed That He Knew Who He Was, It Was Just That He Had to Figure Out How to Be Himself About It, and with His Brother Saying That Although It Might Not Seem Possible Now, Before He Knew It He Wouldn't Be Able to Equate the Way He Dressed and Acted with Who He Was, Even If He Wanted to, Ever Again

Acknowledgments

Thank you to Jenna Johnson and Sara Birmingham for your vision, generosity, and belief, and for everything you've done to grow this work. I'm deeply grateful.

Thank you to Eleanor Jackson for your incredible expertise, savvy, and kindness, every step of the way.

Thanks to the FSG copyediting team for a thorough and insightful review.

Thanks to David Bachmann, Paula Closson Buck, Jeff Glodek, Nathan Graham, Derek Palacio, David Peak, Andrew Roddewig, and Stephen Lloyd Webber for your honest and encouraging feedback on early drafts.

Thank you to Nathan Graham, Michelle Mariano, Derek Palacio, and Claire Vaye Watkins for the gifts of your friendship, literary guidance, and professional advice.

Thank you to Kevin McIlvoy for saying, "Your first assignment will be forty pages of fiction." And for everything that followed, and follows still.

Thank you to Robert Boswell, Antonya Nelson, and Alexander Parsons—again and again.

Thank you to my Creative Writing Program and English Department colleagues at Bucknell University and to my former Writers Institute colleagues at Susquehanna University for your nonstop support and truly inspiring examples. I'm lucky and I know it.

Thank you to Dana Diehl, Melissa Goodrich, Will Hoffacker, and Elizabeth Deanna Morris Lakes.

Thank you to Deirdre O'Connor for the Writer's Boot Camp.

Apologies to Lumans and Dustyn for running that red light.

Thank you to the great Kris Trego for taking the time to share your internationally renowned archaeological expertise (more than once!)—for our discussions, your suggestions, and your generosity as a colleague and a reader of fiction.

Thank you to the dedicated professionals at the Cahokia Mounds State Historic Site, especially Bill Iseminger, for graciously answering a stranger's many questions.

Dziękuję to Joanna Matuszak for the stimulating and enlightening conversation on Eastern European performance art.

Thank you to Victor LaValle for patiently showing me how to make the draft way, way better; to Lance Cleland, for organizing an astounding conference; and to my Tin House workshop-mates: Jennifer Brody, Hope Chernov, Kala Dunn, Jared Lipof, Dorotea Mendoza, Karen Munro, Thirii Myo Kyaw Myint, Loie Rawding, Kawai Washburn, and Janelle Williams, with a special thank-you to Erinn Kindig for that early email.

Thank you to Andrew Roddewig—and to Dick and Noreen Roddewig—for the trip.

Thank you to Jordan Kardasz and Lucy Kim for conversations about Prague.

Thank you to Bart Davis for answering a question about hand-rolled cigarettes.

Thank you to the chombattas, every one of you.

Thank you to Bron Gacki for Polish and Polish-American wisdom.

Thank you to Rus Bradburd and Connie Voisine for your

place in Lincoln Square—for the desk and the chair where most of the first draft of this work was written.

Thank you to my family—the Scapellatos, Gackis, Kostals, Thurmans, Cocos, Martinciches, and Horvaths—especially to my parents, Marge and Frank, for your love, curiosity, and wit, for the wondrous way you live your lives, and for dealing with this dupa jasiu. I love you.

Thank you to Mario Scapellato for reading I don't know how many drafts of this book, and for seeing and saying what I can't, on and off the page.

And thank you to Dustyn, first reader, best friend, for truth, and to Vida, our love, for life.

A NOTE ABOUT THE AUTHOR

Joseph Scapellato published his debut story collection, *Big Lonesome*, in 2017. He earned his MFA in fiction at New Mexico State University and has been published in *Kenyon Review Online*, *Gulf Coast*, *Post Road*, *PANK*, *UNSAID*, and other literary magazines. His work has been anthologized in *Forty Stories*, *Gigantic Worlds*, and *The &NOW AWARDS: The Best Innovative Writing*. Scapellato is an assistant professor of English in the creative writing program at Bucknell University. He grew up in the suburbs of Chicago and lives in Lewisburg, Pennsylvania, with his wife, daughter, and dog.